The Hum

A Novel by

Gimmi Ray

Contents

The Hum

First Edition, 2026

ISBN: 978-1-9193459-0-1 (paperback)
ISBN: 978-1-9193459-1-8 (hardcover)

Published by Hack3d Press | www.hack3d.io

For more **Hack3d Press** books and information,
visit **www.hack3d.io**.

Dedication

For those who bake bread before dawn.
For those who plant trees they will never sit beneath.
For those who hold doors for strangers and never know who follows.
For those who leave more than they take.
For those who sit with the dying when there is nothing left to say.
For those who write letters that may never be answered.

And for my wife.
Who held the lantern while I wandered in the dark.
Who waited while I found my way back.
Who heard the Hum before I learned to write it down.
Every book is built on someone's patience.
This one was built on yours.

Introduction: The Sound of What Did Not Break

We are taught that history is collision.

We are taught that the world is shaped by armies and emperors, by borders inked in blood and erased in ash. We memorize the dates of the battles. We learn the names of the conquerors. We measure the ruins and call it a map of the past.

But there is another history. It is not written in ink. It is hummed.

Press your ear to the world.

Not to the headlines or the speeches, not to the sirens or the stock tickers. Press it lower. Press it to the floorboards of an old house where generations have walked. Press it to the earth beneath a tree that has stood for two centuries. Press it to the chest of someone who loves you, while they sleep.

You will hear it.

Beneath the roar of engines and the silence of satellites, beneath the hum of machines that never rest, there is an older vibration. Four notes, ancient and patient, that have never stopped playing since the first human chose to feed another instead of fight them.

G. D. A. E.

This is the sound of what did not break.

It is the sound of bread shared in darkness, when there was barely enough for one. Of a seed pressed into mud by hands that could not stop shaking. Of a key gripped so tightly it left grooves in the palm, a key to a door that did not yet exist, held by someone who believed it would.

We call it the Hum.

You have heard it before.

Perhaps you did not know what to call it. Perhaps it came to you in the kitchen at midnight, when you could not sleep and found yourself making tea for no one. Perhaps it found you on a park bench, watching a stranger help another stranger with directions, their heads bent together over a phone like two people sharing a secret. Perhaps it was the moment you realized your mother had been standing at your door for ten minutes, not wanting to wake you, just wanting to see you breathe.

The Hum does not announce itself. It does not demand attention. It simply plays, beneath the noise of everything that is trying so hard to be noticed, and it waits for anyone who is quiet enough to hear.

Most of us hear it only in fragments. A note here. A chord there. A stirring in the chest we cannot name, so we let it pass. We return to the noise. We forget.

But some people do not forget.

Some people hear the Hum so clearly that it changes the shape of their lives. It becomes the bass note beneath every decision, the rhythm their hands move to when they do not know they are moving. These people are not saints. They are not heroes in the way the history books mean. They are ordinary, flour-dusted, mud-stained, glass-surrounded, and they do extraordinary things without ever knowing the word for what they have done.

This book is about three of them.

You will meet a baker who discovered that grief, kneaded long enough, rises.

His name was Elian, and he lived in a village that has since been forgotten by every map. He woke at four in the morning, every morning, because that is what bakers do. Not because anyone forced him. Not because he loved the work; some days he hated it, hated the ache in his shoulders and the silence of the kitchen and the empty chair where his brother used to sit. He woke because flour becomes bread only when someone is willing to shape it. He woke because bread becomes food only when it is given away.

He carried an iron key on a nail above the oven. It was meant for a house that would never be built, a cottage at the edge of a meadow, designed by a brother who did not come home from the war. Elian could not bring himself to throw it away. He could not bring himself to use it. So he held it, day after heavy day, until the morning he gave it to a stranger.

That was the morning the Hum found its first vessel.

You will meet a soldier who learned that the only way to bury shame is to plant something in its place.

His name was Henry, and he had walked away from a war that had already walked away from him. He carried almost nothing: a stolen map, a tin of meat he could not open, and an acorn the size of his thumbnail. The acorn was the only whole thing he had seen in three years. Unbroken. Complete. A small brown promise that life could continue from almost nothing.

He heard the Hum drifting through morning fog, and he followed it to a bakery where a stranger gave him bread without asking what he had done to deserve it. He did not deserve it. That was the point. That was the whole point.

Henry planted the acorn in a meadow at the edge of a village. He buried the iron key beside it, a key to a house he had never seen, given to him by a man whose name he did not know. He whispered words into the dark soil, words meant for someone named Thomas, and then he walked into a horizon that held no promises.

He never saw the tree that grew from that planting. He never knew the roots had wrapped themselves around the rusting key, holding it like a secret, waiting for the hand that would one day come to find it.

You will meet an architect who built a cage of glass and shattered it with a key she found in the roots of a tree.

Her name was Clara, and she lived in a city that had forgotten what silence meant. Not the silence of peace, but the silence of absence, the silence of a million people in a million rooms, each one perfectly climate-controlled, perfectly alone. She had not touched another human being in eleven months. She had designed it that way. She had called it optimization.

Then she heard the Hum.

It came to her in a garden she was not supposed to visit, rising from the bark of a tree that should not have existed in that sterile place. She pressed her palm to the wood and felt two centuries of holding: a key buried in the roots, waiting; a song carried through the rings, patient; a vibration that said, without words: *You are not alone. You have never been alone. You are part of a structure so vast and so old that your loneliness is only a forgetting.*

She pried the key from the roots. She did not know whose hand had placed it there. She did not know the name of the baker or the soldier or the tree that had kept the secret for two centuries.

But she heard the four notes. And she began to build anew.

This book is about the architecture the Hum has built.

It is not fragile. It is a structure made of the most durable material in the universe: the decision to remain. A cathedral whose stones are refusals, refusals to release, to surrender, to believe that kindness is naive. Every meal shared with a stranger is a beam. Every hand held in the dark is a buttress, unseen and load-bearing. Every time someone chooses to stay when leaving would be easier, a new room is added to the house that no one can see but everyone can feel.

In these pages, you will not find a world without shadow. You will find a world where shadow is what gives light its edge.

There is grief here. There is war. There is loneliness so sharp it could cut glass. We do not pretend these things do not exist. We do not offer you a fairy tale where pain is just a prelude to a happy ending.

We offer you a harder, more honest truth: the story of what grows through the cracks.

They never met.

The baker died before the soldier found the tree. The soldier vanished before the architect was born. Two centuries stretched between the first loaf of bread and the last shard of glass.

And yet.

They are joined by a force stronger than time: the same four-note song, passed from mouth to mouth, from hand to hand, from one reluctant heart to the next. They are joined by a key that was never used to open a door, because it was the door. They are joined by the decision, made three times in three different centuries, to give something away without knowing where it would land.

This is the history they did not teach you. This is the architecture they cannot raze. This is the story that keeps building itself, brick by brick, every time someone chooses mercy over fear.

Turn the page.

The Hum is already playing.

Chapter 1: The Empty Chair

The flour settled on the table like a held breath.

Elian stood at the wooden table in the gray-blue silence before dawn, hands white to the wrists, shoulders bent under a weight that had nothing to do with the work. The village slept. The cobblestones outside were slick with mist, and the only sounds in the world were the pop and whisper of the fire, the soft exhale of dough rising beneath linen cloths, and the grinding of flour against wood as he pushed the heels of his palms into the mass before him.

Push. Fold. Turn.

The rhythm was older than language. Older than grief. It lived in his hands the way his grandfather's hands had carried it, and his great-grandfather's before that. Four generations of men had stood at this same table, their palms pressing into the same wood, their backs aching in the same places. Elian did not have to think. He only had to move, and the flour would become dough, and the dough would become bread, and the bread would become...

He stopped.

In the corner where the shadows pooled deepest sat an empty chair.

Oak. Notched leg from the year Thomas tried to repair it and cracked the joint instead. Seat worn to a shine by forty years of weight, first their father, who had sat there every morning to watch his sons learn the trade, pipe smoke curling around his head like a wreath. Then Thomas, who would burst through the kitchen door after morning chores with straw in his hair and flour on his coat from brushing too close to the bins. Thomas, who never walked when he could run, never spoke when he could laugh, never sat when he could sprawl.

Thomas, who had once carved their initials into the underside of that chair with his pocket knife, so that even when they were old men they would know: *E & T. Brothers. 1903.*

Now the chair held only air and the specific, crushing heaviness of waiting.

One year. The chair had been empty for exactly one year.

The bakery had been in the family for three generations.

Elian's grandfather had built it with his own hands, stone by stone, when the village was still a cluster of farms and the road was barely more than a cart path. He had set the cornerstone on his wedding day, and his wife had pressed a coin into the mortar for luck. That coin was still there, buried in the wall behind the oven, invisible but present, a secret the building kept.

His father had expanded it, adding the second room where the proving racks stood, the small apartment above where Elian and Thomas had grown up. The smell of bread had been the first thing Elian knew, before he knew his own name. He had learned to walk by holding onto the edge of the kneading table. He had learned to read by tracing the words on flour sacks.

And Thomas, Thomas had been the one who dreamed of more.

We could open a second shop in the city, he used to say. *We could train apprentices. We could write our recipes in a book so that people a hundred years from now could bake the same bread we bake.*

Elian had laughed at him. *You think too big, Thomas.*

Someone has to, Thomas had replied. *You think just the right size. Between the two of us, we'll get it exactly right.*

Between the two of them.

Now Elian baked alone, and the bakery felt too large for one man.

The letter had arrived on a Tuesday.

Elian remembered that detail because it was the same day he had burned the bottom of the rye loaves, something he hadn't done since he was a boy. He had been distracted, watching the road through the window, waiting for the post. He told himself he wasn't hoping. Hoping was dangerous. But his eyes kept drifting to the path, and his hands forgot the fire, and when the knock came, he knew.

Black wax. Official seal. A single page.

Missing and presumed. Three words to erase a life. Three words, and no body to bury, no grave to visit, no bone to hold and say goodbye to. Just a line in a ledger somewhere. Just a statistic.

Just a silence that moved into the bakery and claimed more space than any living man.

Elian had read the letter eleven times. He memorized its punctuation. He held it over the fire more than once, watching the paper curl at the edges, feeling the heat lick at his fingers, and then pulled it back, because even this terrible thing bore his brother's name. Somewhere in the chain of military hands that had passed this paper from trench to telegraph to postal clerk to his door, Thomas's name had been written. Thomas's absence had been recorded. And Elian could not bring himself to destroy the only proof that his brother had existed.

He kept the letter in a drawer beneath the flour bins. He never read it anymore. He didn't have to. The words lived in him now, syllables lodged like stones.

Elian kneaded.

Push. Fold. Turn.

His shoulders burned. Good. Pain was a distraction. Pain was something to do with his hands besides reaching for a chair that would never answer.

The fire crackled, and he listened for sounds the fire could not make. Footsteps on the path. The creak of the door. A voice calling his name in the particular way Thomas had called it, half-teasing, half-tender, always carrying the undertone of a private joke they had shared since childhood.

Nothing. The fire and the flour and the silence.

Above the oven, on a nail driven into the stone, hung the iron key.

Elian did not look at it. He did not have to. He knew exactly how it looked, thick and old-fashioned, hand-forged by the blacksmith on the other side of the village, the handle shaped like a curving vine because Thomas had insisted. *It's not just a key,* Thomas had said. *It's a promise. It should look like something worth keeping.*

Thomas had dreamed of that cottage since before the war. Since the summer of '13, when the world still believed in peace and the village did not yet know what was coming. He had been obsessed with the meadow at the edge of town, a quiet slope where wildflowers grew thick and the light hit the grass at sunset like something from a painting.

That's where it'll be, Thomas had said, standing in that meadow with his arms spread wide. *A cottage with a porch facing east, so we can watch every sunrise. I'll plant a vegetable garden in the back. And there'll be a room just for you, Elian, for when you visit. And when I have children, they'll call you Uncle, and you'll teach them to bake the rye without burning the bottom.*

Elian had laughed then, shaking his head at the audacity of his brother's imagination. Thomas had always treated life as a collection of minor details that he alone possessed the map for.

The key came later, during Thomas's last leave. He had given it to Elian at the train station, the morning he returned to the front. He had pressed it into his brother's palm, cold metal against warm skin, and said: *Hold onto this. When I come back, we build it together.*

When I come back.

Elian lifted the key from its nail.

The metal was cold and pitted now, rough with a year of touching. He held it every morning since the letter arrived. At first while weeping. Then while raging. Then while bargaining with a God he wasn't sure he believed in. Now while numb, which was somehow worse than all the other stages. The grief had become geography. Simply the terrain he lived in.

He pressed the key to his chest, the weight of a promise the world had shattered.

"I am still here, Thomas." He whispered it into the steam rising from the proving bowls. "I am still here."

He did not know if he was reassuring his brother's ghost, or himself.

Outside, the sky was beginning to lighten. A bruised purple along the horizon, then a thin line of gold, then the slow bleed of morning. Soon the village would wake. Soon there would be footsteps and voices and the ordinary noise of people who had not lost everything.

Elian set the key back on its nail. He turned to the dough.

He had stopped baking the spare loaf after Thomas died.

It was a tradition their father had started, always one extra loaf, left on the windowsill for whoever might need it. Travelers. Beggars. Children from the poorer farms who sometimes appeared at dawn with hungry eyes and no coins. The spare loaf was never sold. Simply given, and their father had been fierce about this. *We do not bake for profit alone,* he used to say. *We bake because flour becomes food only when it is shared.*

Thomas had continued the tradition with a convert's zeal. He would place the spare loaf on the sill himself, sometimes adding a piece of cheese or a jar of preserved fruit when there was extra. He believed, with an intensity that Elian had found both touching and naive, that bread was a form of prayer. That every loaf given away was a sentence in a conversation with something larger than himself.

Elian had believed it too, once. Before the war took his brother and returned only a letter. Now he looked at the empty windowsill. Nothing but exhaustion.

What was the point of feeding strangers when the world devoured brothers and returned only paper?

Kindness had begun to feel like a dialect spoken by the naive. Generosity had begun to feel like a trick, a way the universe lured you into hoping so it could enjoy shattering you more completely. Elian baked for the village because it was his trade, because people paid, because he did not know how to do anything else. But the spare loaf, the loaf that was pure gift, pure faith, that he had abandoned.

The windowsill stayed empty. The nail where the spare loaf used to hang stayed bare.

And Elian told himself it didn't matter.

But this morning, something was different.

He did not know what. The fire burned the same. The flour weighed the same. The chair sat empty in its corner, unchanged. But as Elian kneaded, a sound escaped his throat, a low, circular vibration he didn't intend.

Four notes. Rising and falling like breath.

G. D. A. E.

He had not chosen to hum. His body had simply remembered before his mind could intervene.

Thomas's melody. The song Thomas used to whistle when they were boys, crouched in the tall grass behind the mill, pretending the world was a place where brothers lived forever. The song their mother had sung before she died, when Elian was too young to remember but Thomas was old enough to carry. The Hum.

Where had it come from?

Elian did not know. He only knew that his mother had hummed it to Thomas in the last weeks of her life, when the fever had taken her speech but not her voice. Thomas had told him, once, on a summer night when they were both old enough to drink but still young enough to sit on the roof and look at stars:

She hummed it every night. The same four notes. I asked her what it meant, and she couldn't tell me; she was too sick to talk by then. But she smiled. She smiled like the melody was an answer to a question I didn't know how to ask.

Elian had not thought of that conversation in years. But now, in the gray-blue silence of the bakery, the Hum rose from his throat like water from a spring, and he could almost feel his mother's hand on his forehead, his brother's laughter in his ears.

The melody filled the bakery. It filled the spaces between the crackle of fire and the scrape of dough. It filled Elian's chest, and for a moment, just a moment, the weight there shifted. Not lifted. Not healed. But *shifted*, the way a heavy stone shifts when water finds its way beneath.

He looked at the empty chair.

And for one suspended breath, it ceased to be an absence. It became a door, closed, yes, but not locked. Not erased. Waiting for someone to find the key.

Elian's hands moved before he decided.

He reached for the small, extra portion of dough, the portion he had ignored for a year. His fingers sank into the soft mass. The flour clung to his skin.

And without thinking, without deciding, he began to shape.

A braid. Three strands woven tight. One for yesterday. One for today. One for the thing he could not yet name.

Thomas's voice echoed in his memory: *Flour is just sleeping wheat. We wake it so it can feed someone. That's the whole point, Elian. That's the whole point of any of it.*

The braid took shape beneath his hands. He did not know who it was for. He did not know if anyone would come. He only knew that his hands had remembered something his heart had tried to forget, and that the Hum was still humming in his throat, and that for the first time in a year, the air in the bakery felt like it could hold more than grief.

He set the braid on the proving rack, beside the regular loaves. He covered it with a clean cloth, the way his father had taught him. He placed his palm flat on the linen and felt the warmth beneath, the slow, patient heat of dough beginning to rise.

You're doing it again, a voice said in his head. Thomas's voice. *You're baking for someone you don't know. You're giving without counting the cost.*

Elian closed his eyes. His throat tightened.

Is this what you wanted? he asked the silence. *Is this why the melody came back?*

The silence did not answer. Silences never did. But the dough rose beneath his palm, and the fire crackled in the oven, and somewhere in the village, the first rooster began to crow.

He slid the loaves into the fire.

The sun rose.

Purple to gold to white, a white so clean it hurt to look at. The mist burned off the cobblestones. The first shutters creaked open. The village began its slow awakening, the sounds of morning layering over each other like voices joining a song: a baby crying, a dog barking, the clatter of a milk cart on the lane.

Elian stood at the window.

The spare loaf was cooling on the sill, the first one in a year. Steam rose from its crust in thin, wavering lines, carrying the smell of yeast and honey out into the morning air. Anyone passing would see it. Anyone passing would know what it meant: *This is for you. Whoever you are. Whatever you have done. This is for you.*

He did not know if anyone would come. He did not know if kindness would be answered, or if the bread would grow cold and the birds would take it, or if he would stand here for hours watching an empty lane, foolish for having hoped.

But he stood anyway.

He stood with the iron key clutched in his flour-dusted fist, humming the four notes into the stillness of a world that had forgotten how to listen.

He had no way of knowing the sound was traveling. He did not know the key was a seed. He did not know that at the village edge, in the mist rising from the cold ground like breath from a sleeping beast, a man with shaking hands had stopped walking. A man who had heard four notes drifting through the fog and felt his heart, for the first time in three years, remember what it meant to beat.

Elian knew only this: for the first time in a year, the air in the bakery stirred. And somewhere, in the corner where shadows pooled deepest, the empty chair seemed less like an ending and more like a door.

Chapter 2: Brothers

Summer in 1913 was a slow, golden honey.

Elian and Thomas lay in the tall grass at the edge of the meadow, watching clouds drift overhead like ships bound for harbors they would never see. The air was heavy with the smell of wild clover and the steady rasp of grasshoppers. A hawk circled lazily above the tree line, riding thermals, in no hurry to hunt.

Elian was seventeen, a boy who preferred the quiet alchemy of the bakery, the predictable magic of flour and water and heat, the satisfaction of loaves emerging golden from the oven. Thomas, at nineteen, was a man of restless horizons and unbuilt dreams. He was always looking at the edge of things: the edge of the meadow, the edge of the village, the edge of everything he had not yet become.

They were different in almost every way. Elian was steady where Thomas was restless, quiet where Thomas was loud, content where Thomas was hungry. Their father used to say that God had split one soul between them and given each half what the other lacked.

But in this meadow, in this honey-slow afternoon, none of that mattered. They were simply brothers, lying in the grass, watching the sky do nothing.

Thomas sat up, his hair a tangled mess of stalks and sunlight. He pointed to the exact center of the meadow, a spot where the light seemed to rest with particular tenderness.

"There," Thomas said. "That's where it'll be."

"What will?" Elian asked, though he already knew. Thomas had been talking about this meadow for years.

"The house," Thomas said, his voice dropping into the register he used for sacred things. "A cottage with a porch facing east so we can watch the sun rise every single morning. Stone walls, like the bakery, so it'll stand for a hundred years. I'll plant a garden for vegetables out back, tomatoes and beans and those little peppers Mother used to grow. And there'll be a room on the side just for you, for when you visit. And when I have children, they'll call you Uncle Elian, and you'll teach them how to make the rye bread without burning the bottom."

Elian laughed, a sound that felt light in his chest. "You don't even have a wife yet, Thomas."

Thomas grinned, that wide, infectious smile that could make a winter morning feel like July. "Details, Elian. Life is just a set of details waiting for someone to arrange them."

He lay back down, folding his hands behind his head. His eyes were fixed on the clouds, but Elian knew his brother was seeing something else entirely: walls and windows, a hearth and a door, a life that hadn't happened yet.

"Do you ever think about leaving?" Thomas asked.

"Leaving what?"

"The village. The bakery. All of it." Thomas turned his head to look at Elian. "Don't you ever wonder what's out there?"

Elian considered the question. He thought about the road that led out of the village, the one he had never followed past the miller's barn. He thought about the travelers who sometimes stopped at the bakery, their clothes dusty from distant places, their eyes carrying stories he would never hear.

"No," he said finally. "I like it here. I like the bakery. I like knowing what tomorrow will look like."

Thomas nodded slowly. "That's what I mean. You hold things, Elian. You keep them safe. Me, I can't stop reaching for things I haven't touched yet."

He sat up again and began to hum.

It was a four-note melody, low and circular, that seemed to vibrate in the ground beneath them. The notes rose and fell like breath, like the rhythm of a heart at rest.

"Where did you find that song?" Elian asked. "You've been humming it since we were small."

Thomas went quiet. It was a rare stillness, a shadow crossing the bright field of his face. He plucked a blade of grass and twirled it between his thumb and forefinger.

"Mother used to sing it," Thomas said softly. "When we were small. Before she got sick. You were too young to remember."

Elian didn't remember. He had been three when the fever came, and his only memory of their mother was a sense of warmth and the smell of dried lavender. A feeling more than a face. A presence more than a person.

"She would hum it at night," Thomas continued. "When she was putting us to sleep. I used to lie there in the dark and listen, and it felt like... like the whole world was safe. Like nothing bad could happen as long as she was humming."

He was quiet for a moment, the blade of grass still turning between his fingers.

"It's the only thing I have of her," he said. "So I keep it playing. I figured as long as someone is humming it, she isn't really gone. It's like a thread, you see? It connects the before to the after. It connects us to her, and her to whoever came before her, and on and on, back to the beginning of everything."

He looked at Elian, his eyes fierce with a sudden, protective intensity.

"I want you to know it. Really know it. Not just hear it, *carry* it."

Thomas sat up and faced his brother. He placed one hand on Elian's chest, right over his heart.

"Listen," he said. "Don't just hear. Listen with this."

He began to hum. Low at first, barely a vibration. The first note, G, seemed to come from the earth itself, as if Thomas were channeling something older than either of them. Then D, rising like bread in an oven, warm and alive. Then A, the note that made Elian's chest ache without knowing why. And finally E, high and clear, like light breaking through clouds.

"Now you," Thomas said.

Elian tried. The first note came out thin and uncertain, more breath than sound.

"No, no," Thomas laughed. "You're thinking too hard. That's your problem, Elian, you think everything. Stop thinking. Let it come from here." He tapped Elian's chest again. "From the place where you don't have words."

Elian closed his eyes. He thought of the bakery at four in the morning, when the world was still dark and the fire was just beginning to catch. He thought of the silence before the dough started to rise. He thought of his mother, not a memory, but the shape of a memory, the warmth of something he had never quite held.

He hummed.

G. D. A. E.

The notes rose from his throat as if they had been waiting there his whole life. They joined Thomas's voice, wove around it, became something neither of them could make alone.

"There," Thomas whispered, his eyes bright. "You have it now. You'll always have it. Even when I'm not here to remind you."

They lay back in the grass together, the four notes rising and falling between them like breath, like a shared heartbeat. The sun hovered at its zenith, refusing to set. The meadow held them in its palm. And for one afternoon, the future was nothing but golden light and two voices weaving sound into something that would outlast them both.

Elian did not know, then, that he was learning a prayer. He did not know that these four notes would become the only thing that survived the war, the only bridge between the before and the after.

He knew only that his brother's hand was on his shoulder, and the grass was warm beneath them, and the Hum was theirs now, together.

The years between that summer and the war were a blur that Elian would later struggle to recall.

There had been good years. Thomas courting a girl from the next village, a blacksmith's daughter with dark hair and a laugh that carried. Elian taking over more of the bakery as their father's hands began to shake. Long evenings by the fire, the three of them planning the house that Thomas would build, sketching floor plans on scraps of paper, arguing about whether the kitchen should face east or west.

Then the news came from far away. An archduke shot in a city none of them had heard of. Borders redrawn. Treaties invoked. And suddenly the world that had seemed so solid, so permanent, began to crack.

Thomas enlisted before the conscription notices arrived. He said he wanted to choose his own fate, not wait for it to be handed to him. The blacksmith's daughter wept at the station. Elian stood beside her, dry-eyed and numb, watching his brother become a uniform.

❧ ✿ ☙

The train station in 1917 smelled of coal smoke and goodbye.

Four years had passed since that golden afternoon in the meadow, but it might as well have been a lifetime. The world had stopped being made of honey. It was made of iron and mud and loud, barking orders. The newspapers were full of words like *offensive* and *casualties* and *strategic withdrawal*, words that meant nothing and everything at the same time.

Thomas stood on the platform in a uniform that was too big for his shoulders and too stiff for his spirit. He had been home on leave for two weeks, his first leave in eighteen months, and he was leaving again. The blacksmith's daughter was gone now, married to a farmer with flat feet and a medical exemption. She had written Thomas once, a letter full of apologies and explanations about needing someone who would *be there*, someone solid and present. War made people desperate for certainty, and Thomas was anything but certain. He had burned the letter without reply.

But something of the dreamer was still there, somewhere behind the weary eyes. The restlessness had turned into a grim, quiet resolve. Thomas no longer talked about the house in the meadow. He no longer talked about the future at all.

"I have something for you," Thomas said.

He took Elian's hand and pressed something cold and hard into his palm. It was an iron key, heavy, old-fashioned, hand-forged by the blacksmith on the other side of the village. The handle was shaped like a curving vine, delicate and strong.

"I had it made last week," Thomas said. "For the front door. Of the house."

Elian stared at the key. "Thomas..."

"You should keep it," Thomas continued, as if he hadn't heard. "If I keep it, I might lose it in the mud. Everything gets lost in the mud over there. But you're the steady one, Elian. You hold things. I chase things. You keep this for me."

His voice cracked on the last word, and for a moment Elian saw past the uniform, past the weariness, past the years of war. He saw his brother as he had been in the meadow, pointing at the place where his life would begin.

"Hold onto this," Thomas said. "When I come back, we'll build it together."

When I come back.

The train whistle shrieked, a jagged sound that tore through the morning. Soldiers began to board, their movements mechanical, their faces blank. Thomas climbed the steps and found a window seat. His face appeared behind the soot-stained glass, a blur of features Elian had known his whole life.

As the train began to pull away, Elian saw his brother's lips move. He couldn't hear the sound over the roar of the engine, but he knew the shape of the notes. Thomas was humming. He was spinning the thread, connecting the before to the after, refusing to let go.

Elian stood on the platform until the smoke cleared and the tracks were empty, the iron key clutched so tightly it left an imprint on his skin. The last note of the Hum seemed to hang in the air for a long moment, like a question waiting for an answer.

Then it faded, and there was only silence.

Back in the bakery, the memory dissolved into the smell of rising rye.

Elian leaned against the wooden table, his chest rising and falling in time with the heat of the oven. He looked at the iron key in his hand, the same key he had been holding for a year, waiting for a return that would never come.

He understood now why the melody had surfaced this morning, after a year of silence. Why his throat had opened and the four notes had risen without permission.

Thomas was not asking to be mourned. He was asking to be continued.

The Hum was not a lament. It was a foundation. It was the first stone of a house that could still be built, even if the builder never returned. It was the thread that connected the before to the after, the dead to the living, the given to the received.

The spare loaf was nearly ready. Elian could hear the crust crackling in the oven, a tiny, musical sound of life breaking through its shell. Somewhere out there, beyond the bakery door, someone was hungry. Someone was walking through fog, carrying a weight they could not name.

And Elian finally knew what to do with his hands.

He hung the iron key back on its nail. He opened the oven door. And as the heat rushed out to meet him, he began to hum.

The thread was spinning again.

Chapter 3: The Soldier

Henry's hands would not stop shaking.

He buried them deep in the pockets of his greatcoat, but the tremor lived deeper than pockets could reach. It lived in his marrow, in the spaces between his bones, in the place where his body remembered things his mind had tried to forget. It had moved in three years ago, somewhere in the mud of the Somme, and it had never paid rent or asked permission. It simply stayed, a permanent guest in a body that no longer felt like his own.

He was walking. Days, maybe weeks. Time had stopped meaning anything after the first night, when he crossed the line between soldier and something else. Something without a name. Something the army had a word for, a word that lodged in his chest like shrapnel.

Deserter.

He said it to himself sometimes, in the dark, testing its weight. *Deserter.* A man who ran. A coward. A traitor to his country and his comrades and everything he had once believed in.

But that was not quite right, was it?

He did not run. He charged into the fire until charging became reflex. He watched men die so close their blood became part of his uniform. He held a boy from Manchester, nineteen years old, while the boy called for his mother and bled out into the mud. He did everything asked of him, and then more, and then things he would never speak of, not to anyone, not even in the silence of his own mind.

He did not run because he was afraid. He ran because one morning, standing in a trench that reeked of rot and cordite, he understood: the noise had finally broken something structural. Some load-bearing wall in the architecture of his mind had cracked, and if he stayed one more hour, he would collapse into a shape that could never be rebuilt.

So he walked. Into trees. Into fog. Into a silence that felt like the first breath after drowning.

He carried a canvas bag over his shoulder.

Inside: a stolen map, its creases worn soft from folding and unfolding. A tin of meat he could not bring himself to open. A flask of water, half-empty. A wool blanket, threadbare and stinking of smoke.

And an acorn.

The acorn was the size of his thumbnail. He had found it in a forest near the border, three days after he crossed the line. He had been walking through trees that reminded him of home, proper trees, not the splintered stumps of no-man's-land, when he came upon a clearing.

The light there was different. Soft. Golden. It fell through the canopy in thick shafts, and in one of those shafts, on a bed of moss and fallen leaves, lay the acorn.

Perfect. Unbroken. Not a crack, not a blemish.

Henry stopped walking. He stood at the edge of the clearing and stared at the acorn as if it were a miracle. And perhaps it was. In three years, he had seen bodies and mud and metal. Men reduced to meat, buildings reduced to rubble, entire landscapes reduced to moonscapes of craters and wire. Everything broken. Everything rotting. Everything ground down to its component parts and scattered in the wind.

But this acorn was *whole*. Complete. A small brown promise that life could begin again from almost nothing.

He picked it up. Warm from the sun, warmer than anything he had touched in months. He held it in his palm. Its weight was negligible by any measure, but to Henry the heaviest thing in the world. The weight of possibility. The weight of a future he could not yet imagine.

He put it in his pocket. He had carried it ever since.

Some nights, when sleep refused to come and the dark pressed in like water, Henry would take the acorn out and hold it to his ear.

He swore he could hear it breathing.

Not literally, of course. He was not mad, or if he was, he was not that kind of mad. But when he held the acorn close and let the silence settle, he could almost hear a pulse, faint and insistent, the quiet insistence of a seed that knew it would become a tree if only someone would give it a chance.

He began to talk to it. Not out loud, but in his mind. He told it about the places he had been. He told it about the men he had known, the ones who had died and the ones who had survived and the ones whose fates he would never learn. He told it about his brothers, three of them, all younger, all still in England, all probably wondering where he was.

He told it about the boy from Manchester.

He was your age, Henry said to the acorn in his mind. *He had freckles and a gap between his front teeth, and he told me his mother made the best meat pies in all of England. He said when the war was over, he would take me to her shop and buy me one. He said we would sit in her kitchen and eat until we could not move, and we would laugh about all the things that had tried to kill us and failed.*

Henry held the acorn tighter.

He died calling for her. And I could not do anything. I held him and he died, and I could not do anything.

The acorn did not answer. But it stayed warm in his palm, and that was enough.

Now, at the edge of a village he did not know, Henry stood in the morning mist and tried to remember what belonging felt like.

The fog was thick enough to lean against. It muffled everything: sound, sight, thought. The world had shrunk to shapes and whispers. The shadow of a fence post. The distant crow of a rooster that knew nothing of war. The soft percussion of his own footsteps on packed earth.

He did not know where he was. The map had become useless two days ago, when he realized he had crossed into territory it did not cover. He was somewhere in the borderlands, somewhere between the country he had fled and the country he had no right to enter. A man without a nation. A soldier without a war.

He was certain that anyone who saw him would recognize what he was. They would see the hollow in his eyes, the tremor in his hands, the mud ground into his uniform. They would see *deserter* branded on his forehead. They would call for the authorities, and the authorities would send him back. Back to the trenches, back to the noise, back to the place where the boy from Manchester had died in his arms.

He could not go back. He would rather die in this fog than go back.

Then he heard it.

A sound. Drifting through the gray like smoke, like the ghost of something he had lost so long ago he had forgotten he was missing it.

Four notes. Ancient and patient. Rising and falling like breath.

G. D. A. E.

Henry stopped.

The fog seemed to thin around him, as if the sound were burning it away. The notes came again, clearer now, and something stirred in his chest. Something that had been sleeping for three years, buried so deep he had forgotten it existed.

His heart, which had been a frantic arrhythmic thing for months, found a rhythm. Slowed. Steadied. Began to beat in time with the sound.

He followed the melody without deciding to. His feet moved before his mind could object, carrying him toward the source of the music. The fog parted like a curtain, and there, glowing in the gray morning like a lantern in a shipwreck, stood a bakery.

Small. Stone walls thick with age, the color of old honey. A chimney exhaling smoke in lazy spirals. A wooden door, slightly ajar. And the windows. The windows burned with a golden light so warm, so honest, that Henry felt it on his skin like the first sun after a long winter.

The smell came next. Bread. Not the hard stale rations of the trenches, dense as stone and tasting of nothing. Real bread, yeasty and alive, crusted with heat, carrying the promise that somewhere in this broken world, people still woke before dawn to make beautiful things.

Henry stepped out of the fog and into the edge of the light.

He stood in the alley shadows and looked at his hands.

They were gray. Stained with the permanent grime of trenches, mud worked so deep into his fingerprints it would never leave. The nails were cracked and black. The knuckles were raw from cold and work and violence. These were the hands of a man who had dug graves. Who had held dying friends. Who had done things he would never speak of, not even to himself.

These hands did not belong in light.

He pressed himself against cold stone and watched the baker move behind the golden window. A young man, perhaps twenty-two or twenty-three, with flour-dusted arms and a face that carried the weight of some private sorrow. He worked alone, kneading dough with the steady rhythm of someone who had done this a thousand times before. And he was humming.

The same four notes. Over and over. As if stitching the air together with sound.

Henry reached into his bag and touched the acorn. Smooth and cool. A small weight of possibility in a pocket full of shame.

I cannot go back, he thought. *I cannot return to the noise. But I do not know how to go forward. I do not know how to be a person anymore. I do not know how to stand in the light without the light seeing what I have become.*

He did not move. Could not. He was caught between the darkness of the alley and the glow of the window, a figure made of shadow, waiting for the world to decide whether he deserved to exist.

The baker's hands kept moving. *Push. Fold. Turn.* The rhythm was ancient, patient, indifferent to war. The Hum kept playing, four notes rising and falling, a melody that did not care what Henry had done or failed to do. It simply played, the way the sun simply rose, the way the seasons simply turned.

And somewhere beneath the mud and the shame and the tremor in his hands, something in Henry began to remember.

Not hope. Not yet. Something smaller. A recognition that warmth still existed. That bread still rose. That somewhere in the world, a man could stand in a kitchen at four in the morning and hum a melody for no one but himself, and the melody could drift through fog and find a broken soldier in an alley, and the soldier could stand there listening, and nothing bad would happen.

Nothing bad would happen.

Henry stood in the shadows and let the Hum wash over him. He did not step into the light. Not yet. But he stayed. He listened. He let his heart beat in time with the melody.

And in his pocket, the acorn seemed to grow warmer, as if it too were listening, as if it too were beginning to believe that something might yet grow from all this ruin.

Chapter 4: The Exchange

The bakery door opened with a sound like a sigh.

A heavy door, built of oak planks thick enough to stop an arrow, hung on iron hinges that had outlasted three blacksmiths. Usually, it groaned. Usually, it announced every arrival and departure with a rusted complaint that echoed through the shop. But this morning, it swung inward with a strange, breathless hush, as if the wood itself were holding its breath.

Elian lifted the braided loaf from the windowsill and stepped into the morning.

He held it in his hands like an offering. The crust was still too hot to touch comfortably, burning the callouses on his palms, but he did not shift his grip. The heat was grounding. Real. The only solid thing in the world.

He did not look down the street toward the market square, where the early risers would soon be setting up their stalls, stacking crates of apples and turnips, complaining about the frost. He did not look toward the hills, where the sun was fighting its way through the mist.

He looked toward the alley.

He knew someone was there.

He could not have explained how he knew. He was not a man given to premonitions or flights of fancy. He was a baker. He dealt in weights and measures, in temperatures and timings. But the Hum had been too insistent today. It had vibrated in his chest while he kneaded, hummed in his ears while he shaped, pulled at him while he waited for the crust to brown. It felt less like a memory and more like a summons. As if the song were a fishing line cast into the dark, and now, finally, there was a tug on the other end.

As if the bread in his hands had been baked for a specific hunger he could not name.

He crossed the street. His boots rang on the cobblestones, a sharp, lonely sound in the quiet air. The mist swirled around his ankles, cold and damp, smelling of river water and wet stone.

The shadow in the alley moved.

Not a ghost. Not a trick of the light. A man.

Henry was pressed against the rough stone wall like a man trying to dissolve into the architecture. He had pulled his greatcoat tight around him, but it was too thin for this weather, worn threadbare at the elbows and hem. He was tall, but he held himself hunched, shoulders drawn in as if expecting a blow. His face was gaunt, the skin stretched tight over cheekbones sharp enough to cut, and his eyes, his eyes were wide dark pools of a terror so old it had become the only thing he knew.

Elian stopped three feet away.

He did not speak. He did not need to. He knew that look. He saw it every morning, in the mirror above the washbasin, in the hollows beneath his own eyes. The look of a man who has reached the end of his endurance and found that the road keeps going.

The soldier stared at him. He did not run. He seemed frozen, pinned by the sudden reality of being seen. He looked at the bread in Elian's hands, at the steam rising from the golden braid, carrying the scent of yeast and honey into the cold air, and his throat worked. He swallowed, once, twice, a dry, painful clicking sound.

Elian looked at the coat. Military issue, gray wool, stained with mud that looked different from the mud of the village. Darker. Heavier.

"My brother Thomas had a coat like that," Elian said finally. His voice was quiet, without accusation. A statement of fact, dropped into the space between them like a stone into a well. "He never came back to wear it."

The soldier flinched. A small movement, a tightening of the jaw, a flicker of the eyelids, but to Elian it looked like a physical blow. The man's breath hitched. He looked down at his own hands, which were buried deep in his pockets, shaking so hard the fabric of the coat trembled.

"I should not be here," the soldier whispered. His voice was a ruin, rough, unused, scraping against the silence.

"No one should be where they are right now," Elian replied. "The world has lost its way. But you are here. And the bread is warm. So take it."

He took a step forward. He held out the loaf.

The soldier stared at it as if it might be a trap. As if it might be a weapon. As if kindness were a danger he had forgotten how to navigate. He did not take his hands out of his pockets. He pressed his back harder against the stone, as if trying to push through the wall and vanish into the building behind him.

"I can't pay you," the soldier said. "I have nothing."

"I didn't ask for payment," Elian said. "Bread isn't sold at this hour. It's given. It's the rule."

"The rule?"

"My father's rule. My brother's rule. Now mine." Elian shifted the loaf slightly. "It's getting cold. Bread shouldn't be cold. It's an insult to the yeast."

A ghost of a smile touched the soldier's lips, or maybe it was just a tic, a muscle jumping in his cheek. But he moved. Slowly, agonizingly slowly, he pulled his hands from his pockets.

They were shaking violently. They were stained gray with grime, the knuckles raw and bleeding, the nails black. They were hands that had done terrible things, or had terrible things done to them.

Elian did not look away. He did not flinch. He stepped closer, closing the last distance between them, and gently, as if approaching a wounded animal that might bite out of fear, he placed the warm bread into the soldier's hands.

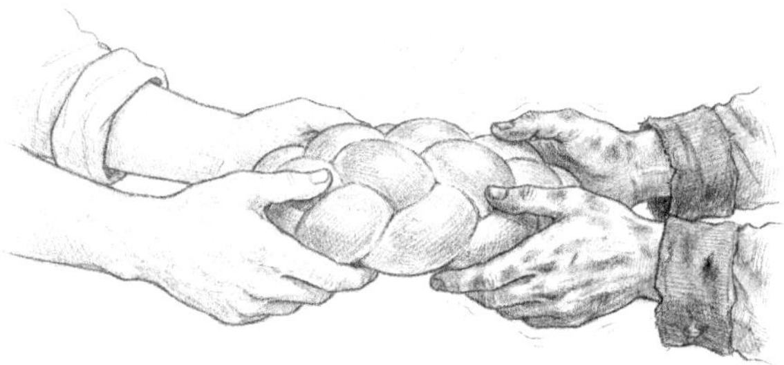

The man's fingers closed around it.

The heat of the loaf traveled into his skin. Elian saw the shock of it register in his eyes, the sudden, undeniable reality of warmth. For a moment, just a heartbeat, the tremor in his hands went still.

They stood like that, connected by a loaf of bread, two strangers joined by the simple physics of giving and receiving. The mist curled around them. The sun crested the hill, sending a long, pale finger of light down the alley floor.

Henry looked at the bread. He lifted it to his face and inhaled. The smell broke him. Not just flour and salt. Safety. It smelled of a kitchen where nothing bad had ever happened. It smelled of a morning that wasn't trying to kill him.

He looked at Elian, and his eyes were wet.

"Thank you," he choked out.

"It's just bread," Elian said.

"No," Henry said. "It isn't."

Elian nodded. He understood. It was never just bread.

He reached into his pocket. His fingers brushed the cold, pitted surface of the iron key.

He carried it for a year. Three hundred and sixty-five days of weight. Three hundred and sixty-five mornings of waking up to the heavy, cold lump of it against his hip. For a house that would never be built. For a door that would never be hung. For a brother who would never come home to turn it in the lock.

It was the heaviest thing he owned. Heavier than grief. Heavier than memory. Heavier than the silence in the bakery where Thomas's laugh used to live.

He had thought he was keeping it safe. He had thought he was honoring Thomas by holding onto it. But standing here, in the cold alley with a man who was shaking apart, Elian realized the truth.

He wasn't keeping it safe. He was keeping it dead.

A key is not meant to be held. It is meant to open something. And if the door it was made for no longer existed, then it had to find a new door. Or it had to be given to someone who knew how to build one.

"Take this too," Elian said.

He pulled the key out. It looked dark and ugly in the morning light, a piece of old iron that had forgotten its purpose.

Henry looked at the key, then at Elian. His face was a confusion of fear and wonder. He shifted the bread to one arm, cradling it against his chest like an infant, and held out his shaking hand.

"What is it?"

"A key," Elian said. "My brother Thomas had it made. Before he went back."

"Left for where?"

"The same place you came from," Elian said.

Henry flinched again. He looked down at the key as if it might burn him.

"I carried it for a year," Elian continued, his voice rough. He forced the words out, pushing them past the lump in his throat. "It was for a house he planned to build. A cottage. By the meadow. He drew the plans. He talked about the garden. He told me to hold it for him."

He stopped. He looked at the soldier's gray face, at the mud on his coat, at the way he held the bread as if it were the only anchor in a storm.

"He didn't come back," Elian said. "The house will never exist. And I cannot..." He swallowed hard. "It is too heavy. I cannot carry it anymore. It's pulling me down. I need someone else to take it. Perhaps you can find a use for it. Perhaps you can build something I cannot."

He pressed the iron key into the soldier's open palm.

Cold metal met warm, dirt-stained skin. A year of grief passed from one hand to another. And in that passing, something cracked open, not just between the two men, but in the fabric of the morning itself. The air seemed to shimmer. The Hum, which had been a low vibration in Elian's chest, suddenly swelled, a chord struck on a giant instrument.

The soldier looked at the key. He closed his fingers over it. He held it tight, tighter than he had held the bread.

"I don't have a house," Henry said. "I don't have anything."

"You have a key," Elian said. "That's a start."

Henry looked at Elian. For the first time, he really looked at him. He saw the flour in his hair, the lines of exhaustion around his eyes, the way his shoulders slumped as if a great weight had just been lifted from them. He saw a man who was also breaking, also lost, also searching for a reason to keep breathing.

"I will keep it safe," the soldier said. His voice was stronger now. Not much, but enough. "I do not know what I will do with it. I do not know where I am going. But I will keep it safe."

"That is enough," Elian said. "That is more than enough."

He stepped back. The transaction was complete. The bread was given. The key was passed. The architecture had begun, though neither of them knew what they were building.

"Eat," Elian said. "Before it gets cold."

He turned and walked back toward the bakery. He did not look back. He had given away the thing anchoring him to the dark. For the first time in a year, his pockets were empty, and he felt light enough to float.

Behind him, in the alley, Henry held the bread and the key and tried to remember how to breathe.

He walked out of Oakhaven.

He did not know where he was going, only that he needed to be away from the stone walls, away from the eyes of the village that was waking up. He walked until the cobblestones gave way to dirt, and the dirt gave way to grass.

He stopped at the edge of the meadow.

The mist was lifting here, revealing a field of tall, frost-silvered grass that rippled in the wind like water. It was quiet. A hawk circled overhead. The sun was just clearing the trees, turning the frost into a million tiny diamonds.

Henry sat down in the grass. His legs gave way, and he sat hard, the canvas bag thumping against his side.

He ate the bread.

He ate it slowly, deliberately, tearing off small chunks and letting them dissolve on his tongue like a benediction. He tasted the flour. He tasted the salt. He tasted the heat of the fire and the patience of the hands that had made it. The first food in months that did not taste like survival. It tasted like mercy.

It filled him. Not just his stomach, but the hollow places in his chest where the fear lived. It pushed the cold out. It reminded his blood that it was still moving.

When the bread was gone, he wiped the crumbs from his mouth. No longer a ghost. A man. A tired man, a broken man, but a man who had received something he hadn't earned, and who now had to decide what to do with the gift.

He reached into his canvas bag. His fingers brushed the cool, smooth surface of the acorn.

He pulled it out.

He looked at the key in his other hand.

A seed and a door. A beginning and an ending.

Or perhaps... perhaps they were the same thing. Perhaps every ending was just a seed waiting to be buried properly so it could become something else.

Henry looked at the meadow. He imagined a house standing here. Not a grand house, just a cottage. Stone walls. A porch facing east. A garden in the back. A place where a man could sit and watch the sun rise and not be afraid.

He didn't know how to build a house. He didn't know if he would ever stop shaking long enough to stack stone on stone. But he knew he couldn't keep carrying these things. The acorn was too heavy with potential. The key was too heavy with memory.

He had to put them down.

Henry knelt in the center of the meadow. The grass was wet against his knees. His hands, for once, were steady. He dug into the dark, cold earth with his bare fingers. He felt the soil pack beneath his nails, smelled the mineral richness of ground that had never known war, never known trenches, never drank blood.

He dug a small hole. Just deep enough.

He placed the acorn in the hole. It sat there, small and brown and perfect, a tiny planet in a universe of dirt.

Then, with a tenderness he didn't know he still possessed, he laid the iron key beside it.

Metal against seed. Iron against wood. The made thing and the grown thing, resting together in the dark.

"For Thomas," he whispered. The name was strange on his tongue, a name he had only heard once, but it was right. "For the house that will grow instead."

He covered them both. He scooped the loose earth back into the hole and patted it down. He smoothed the grass over the spot until it looked like nothing had ever happened there.

He stood up. He adjusted his pack. He looked toward the horizon, where the sun was finally breaking through in long, golden shafts that lit the meadow like a stage.

Lighter. The bag was lighter. His pockets were lighter. The crushing weight of his own existence had drained away into the earth, leaving him empty but clean.

Deep beneath the meadow, the acorn and the key settled into the dark. One was a promise of life. The other was a record of loss. Together, they formed the first pillar of an architecture that would take two centuries to complete.

The seed began to drink.

The key began to rust.

And the Hum, carried on the breath of a grieving baker, remained in the wind, patient as a song that knows it will eventually be heard.

Henry turned and began to walk. He didn't know where he was going. But for the first time in three years, he wasn't running away. He was walking toward.

Interlude: The Watcher

Time, to an oak, is not a river but a breath.

It is a slow, rhythmic expansion of the self, a single inhalation that can span decades, an exhalation that scatters a thousand potential lives across the soil. I do not count the passage of existence by the ticking of clocks or the turning of pages. I count it by the deepening ache of winter in my sap, by the weight of the air before a summer storm, and by the slow, inevitable drift of the constellations across the hole in the sky I have spent two centuries trying to fill.

Roots learn to grip. Bark learns to hold. I have taken more than ten breaths now, and with each one, the world has become a louder, thinner place.

The seasons taught me patience.

Spring arrived first as a trembling, a loosening in the frozen soil that crept upward through my roots like a whispered promise. Ice released its grip on the meadow, and the first crocuses pushed through the mud, their purple heads nodding in the rain. I felt my sap begin to rise, that sweet, slow pressure building in my trunk, and I understood for the first time that growing was a kind of joy. The rain tasted of minerals and melted snow, of iron from distant mountains and salt from seas I would never see.

Summer came heavy and golden, pressing the meadow flat with heat. Bees hummed in the clover. Children ran barefoot through the grass, their laughter high and bright as birdsong, and sometimes they climbed my lower branches, wrapping their small arms around my trunk. I learned the particular weight of a child's body, the scrape of fingernails on bark, the way they whispered secrets to me that they would not tell another soul. I kept those secrets. I keep them still.

Autumn painted me in fire. My leaves turned amber, then crimson, then the deep rust of dried blood, and the wind carried them away across the meadow in spiraling dances. Acorns fell from my branches, thudding softly into the soil, each one carrying the possibility of a forest. Most would not survive. Squirrels would bury them and forget. Frost would crack their shells. But a few, a precious few, would find the right patch of darkness and begin the long work of becoming.

Winter taught me stillness. The cold sank into my heartwood, and my sap slowed to a crawl, and I stood bare against the gray sky, a skeleton of branches reaching toward nothing. Snow piled on my limbs, heavy and white, and I bore it. That is what trees do. We bear. The meadow fell silent. Even the crows stopped visiting. And in that silence, I could hear the key dreaming in my roots, its iron voice muffled by rust and time.

Two hundred winters. Two hundred springs. The seasons blurred into a single, endless rhythm, a heartbeat so slow that humans mistook it for stillness.

I remember the planting.

I remember the heat of the man's thumb as he pressed me into the dark, welcoming cool of the earth. I remember the salt of his tears, which tasted of ancient oceans and fresh bread. I remember the vibration of his voice, a low, cracked whisper that carried a name I have held ever since: *Thomas*.

And I remember the key.

The key sank slowly into my roots, rusting into permanence, becoming part of my blood. Cold at first, a foreign weight in the center of my being. But I did not reject it. I chose it. I cradled the iron in my roots the way a mother cradles a sleeping child, shielding it from the rain and the worms and the endless hunger of decay. It became my secret heart, a gift I was not meant to use, but to guard.

The rust came slowly, a chemical patience that matched my own. Year by year, the key's sharp edges softened. Its surface grew rough, pitted, the color deepening from gray to amber to the deep red-brown of old blood. Iron becomes earth, given time. Everything does. But the shape remained. The meaning remained. I could feel the warmth still locked inside it, the memory of the baker's palm, the soldier's tears, the name whispered into soil.

I have kept the door safe. I have grown around it until it is more me than itself.

Around my meadow, the world accelerated.

It happened so slowly that the humans did not seem to notice, but to me, it was a frantic, blurring transformation. First the roads. The cobblestones of the village, warm gray stones that had been worn smooth by generations of feet, vanished beneath a river of black asphalt that smelled of tar and burning. The asphalt was hot when it came, steaming in the rain, and it sealed the earth away from the sky like a wound being sutured closed.

Then the buildings. The stone cottages fell first, the ones with thatched roofs and gardens full of peas and lavender. I had known those cottages since my sapling years. I had felt the vibrations of laughter through the soil, the weight of woodsmoke settling on my leaves. They smelled of bread and wool and centuries. Men came with machines that roared like wounded animals, and the cottages became rubble, and the rubble became dust, and the dust blew away on winds that no longer smelled of anything at all.

Brick rose in their place. Then concrete. Then steel. Each material colder than the last, each one further from the earth. And finally, glass. Towers of glass that climbed higher than I could reach, their surfaces reflecting a sky I could no longer see. They stole my sunlight. They blocked the stars. They hummed with a frequency that made my leaves curl at the edges, a constant, mechanical whine that had nothing to do with music.

The meadow shrank. The fence posts rotted away. The wild clover was choked out by manicured lawns, which were then choked out by the gray, unyielding shadow of towers.

The sky, once a map of stars where I could trace my ancestry, filled with lights that never dimmed and signals that never stopped screaming. The humans stopped looking up. They stopped listening. They forgot how to stand still.

The bakery was the last to go.

I felt it happen from across the village, a trembling in the soil that traveled through root networks until it reached me. The old stone walls that had held Elian's grief, the ovens that had baked bread for Henry, the doorway where a soldier had wept and a baker had forgiven. Machines ate it all. The building did not fall; it was devoured. And where it had stood, glass rose, smooth and featureless, reflecting nothing but its own emptiness.

I mourned in the way trees mourn, which is to say I dropped my leaves early that year, and they fell in a perfect circle around my trunk, and I stood bare through an autumn that should have been golden.

But I remembered.

I watched them move faster and faster, their faces bent toward glowing rectangles, their ears stoppered with wire, their hands forever reaching for something they could never quite touch. They became like ghosts to me, brief, flickering intensities that appeared and disappeared in the space of a single leaf-turn.

I know the weight of a child's foot and the weight of a builder's saw. I know the grip of a grandfather's palm showing bark to small fingers. I know the questions they ask, *how old is this tree?*, and the answer they cannot hear.

Most visitors do not notice. They see only wood and shade. But sometimes, someone stops. Stills. Listens with more than ears. I call this *the full silence,* when a human becomes quiet enough to hear the world breathing. It happens rarely. Once a decade, perhaps. Once a lifetime.

The Hum lived in my fibers.

Faint now. Almost inaudible. Buried beneath the roar of the city that has grown around the meadow like a shell around a pearl. But it is there. Four notes, patient and circular, vibrating through my heartwood at a frequency the machines cannot detect.

G. D. A. E.

I did not know what the sound meant, only that it was a summons. Someone had pressed it into the soil with a song in his throat, and I absorbed the sound, and I have held it ever since.

I am dying now.

Not quickly, trees do not die quickly, but inevitably. I can feel the poison in the soil, the chemical thirst that the rain can no longer quench. The glass towers have stolen my sun. My branches reach for a light that is always filtered, always second-hand. My leaves grow thinner each spring, my bark more brittle.

I am losing the long war against the world that has forgotten I exist.

And yet.

Deep in my roots, the key remains. The Hum still plays. I understand now, in the wordless way that trees understand, that I am not merely a tree anymore. I am a vessel. A reliquary. A living monument to an act of love that predated the glass and the wires and the silence.

I will not let the key be forgotten.

I have been waiting. Not for rescue, but for recognition. For the footsteps that would come, eventually, to find what was hidden in my roots. This is the nature of trees: we are made of waiting. Our rings are years of patience laid one upon another. Our roots are questions planted in darkness, reaching toward answers we may never find.

I will hold until someone comes. Until someone stops long enough to listen. Until someone kneels in the poisoned soil and touches the bark and hears, finally, the four-note song that has been waiting all along for the right pair of ears.

The loneliness has been the hardest part.

Humans do not understand tree-loneliness. They think we are content in our stillness, satisfied with sunlight and rain. But I have known connection. I have felt the baker's tears on my roots. I have heard the soldier's song pressed into my fibers. I have held a key that carries the warmth of hands that loved, and I have watched the world forget that such warmth ever existed.

There were decades when no one touched me at all. When the meadow was fenced off and the signs said KEEP OUT and the children stopped climbing. I stood alone in the shadow of towers, surrounded by millions of heartbeats, and not one of them paused long enough to hear mine. The silence was not peaceful. An ache, a hollowness in my heartwood where connection should have been.

I can feel her now.

She is 102 floors above the ground, encased in a cage of glass. Her heart beats differently than the others, slower, sadder, more like the rhythm of a tree. I have been sensing her for weeks, the way you might sense a storm building on the horizon. A pressure in the air. A gathering. Her footsteps in the tower send vibrations down through steel and concrete and into the poisoned soil, and I feel each one, faint as the brush of a falling leaf.

She is coming. She does not know yet. She thinks she is looking for silence. But she is looking for the key.

She is the one who will find the door.

When she touches my bark, I will exhale the century. I will give her the sound the man pressed into the soil when he planted me. I will hand her the promise that has been dreaming in my roots.

She will not understand at first. Humans rarely do. They think in words, in categories, in things that can be named and filed away. But the Hum is older than language. It is the sound of kindness passing from hand to hand, generation to generation, surviving everything designed to destroy it. She will hear it, and something in her will remember, and that will be enough.

Four notes. A gift passed from root to root, from year to year, from the grieving hands of a baker to the trembling fingers of an architect who does not yet know she is about to rebuild the world.

The Hum does not belong to me. I am only the door it has been waiting behind.

The city roars. The years pass. But the morning is coming. I can feel the shift in the air, the way you feel dawn before you see it. The temperature dropping toward that hour when only bakers are awake, when the world is quiet enough to remember what it has forgotten.

I can feel the weight of her footsteps approaching.

Two hundred years I have waited. I can wait a few hours more.

And when she comes, when her palm presses against my bark and her breath catches in her throat, I will give her everything. The key. The song. The name that has been dreaming in my roots since a grieving man knelt in this meadow and planted hope in the shape of an acorn.

Thomas.

For Thomas.

The circle will complete. The bread will rise. And the Hum will find its way home.

I am ready to exhale.

Chapter 5: The Glass Cage

Clara lived on the 102nd floor, where the air was filtered and the silence was perfect.

She had not touched another human being in eleven months. This was not unusual in the City of Glass. Touch was inefficient, a vector for contamination, a breach in the membrane of the self. The city had solved the problem of loneliness by eliminating the conditions that made it visible. Every apartment was a perfect cube of white space.

Every meal arrived through a slot that opened and closed without human hands. Every surface was smooth, cool, and incapable of holding a fingerprint.

Clara designed these surfaces.

She was an Architect of Flow, one of the city's elite spatial engineers, her work measured not in beauty but in velocity. Her job was to ensure that people moved through buildings without stopping. Friction was the enemy. Lingering was a design flaw. Her masterpiece was the Lumen Corridor, a transit hub so perfectly calibrated that the average pedestrian passed through in 4.2 seconds, a full 1.8 seconds faster than any competing design.

She had won awards. She had stood on stages and accepted crystal plaques while holograms applauded. She had never been embraced.

Her apartment was a reflection of her mind: sparse, elegant, and terrified of chaos. The walls were made of smart-glass that adjusted opacity based on her biometric stress levels. The furniture floated on magnetic fields to make cleaning effortless. There were no photographs. There were no knick-knacks. There was nothing to suggest that a human being lived there, only that a human being was being stored there until needed.

Clara moved through her life like a ghost haunting a machine. She woke at 0600. She consumed her nutrient pack at 0615. She entered the immersion pod at 0630 to begin her work cycle. She designed spaces where no one would ever want to stay, and she did it better than anyone else.

But lately, the silence had fractured.

Not a noise. A feeling, a vibration beneath the floorboards, a hum in the filtered air. A note she could not tune out. A frequency her walls could not filter. It made her skin itch. It made her chest ache with a hunger that the nutrient packs could not satisfy.

She moved through perfection like a ghost looking for a door she couldn't find.

The morning it happened, the light was gray-white.

This was the default setting for Sector 7: Optimal Productivity Spectrum. It was the color of efficiency. The color of nothing.

Clara stood at the window wall of her apartment, looking down at the city. From this height, the streets were just lines of light, the people invisible data points moving along predetermined paths. It was beautiful in the way a circuit board is beautiful: complex, orderly, and dead.

But this morning, there was a flaw in the grid.

A small thing, barely a pixel in the vast resolution of the city. A dark smudge, far below in the Redundant Zone, disrupting the clean geometry of the lower levels. It didn't move. It didn't glow. It simply sat there, absorbing the light around it like a bruise.

Clara pressed her palm against the glass. It was always body-temperature. It never felt like anything.

"Aura," she said. "Magnify Sector 7-B. Coordinates 44-North."

The glass rippled and zoomed. The smudge resolved into shape.

A tree.

Clara stared. She had seen trees before, of course. The vertical farms were full of them, genetically modified oxygen-producers grown in hydroponic gel, their roots tangled in nutrient mesh, their leaves perfectly symmetrical. Those trees were green machines. They were useful.

This tree was different.

Massive. Ancient. Its bark was dark as dried blood, gnarled and twisted in ways that no algorithm would have permitted. Its branches reached out in wild, inefficient directions, grasping at empty air. It looked messy. It looked stubborn. It looked wrong.

And it was standing in a circle of exposed earth, actual dirt, brown and raw, surrounded by the sleek, buckled polymer of a construction site.

Clara felt a strange sensation in her fingertips. A tingle. A phantom memory of texture.

Her display chimed, a soft, polite sound that made her jump.

Site survey required. Sector 7-B. Biological obstruction delaying foundation work. Your expertise requested.

Clara looked at the message. Then she looked back at the tree. It shouldn't be there. The city's zoning laws were absolute. Biological matter was confined to the Preservation Domes. A tree this size, in an uncontrolled zone, was an impossibility.

"Accept," she whispered.

The elevator ride down took four minutes.

A smooth, silent descent through the strata of the city. Clara watched the light change through the transparent doors. The sterile white of the Residential Tier gave way to the amber glow of the Commercial Ring, then the blue pulse of the Data Core.

Layer by layer, the city grew darker. The air grew heavier. The silence lost its perfection and began to fray at the edges.

When the doors opened on the Ground Level, the smell hit her first.

The air was different. Not the recycled, sanitized air of the upper floors. Damp. Musty. It smelled of stagnant water and cold stone and an earthen richness she couldn't name.

Clara stepped out.

The Redundant Zone was a graveyard of old infrastructure. Concrete pillars, cracked and stained, held up the gleaming city above. Cables hung from the ceiling like vines. The light here was dim and flickering, cast by emergency strips that buzzed like trapped insects.

She followed the coordinates on her display. Her footsteps echoed on the wet pavement, too loud in the gloom. She passed construction drones hovering in standby mode, their red eyes pulsing slowly.

And then she saw it.

The tree stood in a circle of light carved out by the construction floodlamps. Up close, it was terrifying. It was so big. The trunk was a wall of rough, scarred wood, wide enough to hide a room inside. The roots had smashed through the polymer walkway, buckling the synthetic stone as if it were cardboard.

"Ma'am?"

Clara started. A man was standing near the perimeter, holding a tablet. He wore the yellow vest of a Site Manager, but he looked young and tired.

"I'm the Architect," Clara said. Her voice sounded thin in the cavernous space.

"Thank the Code," the manager said. "We're stuck. The cutters won't go through. The roots are too deep, and we've hit... something else."

"Something else?"

"Metal. At the base. It's interfering with the drone sensors. The whole grid is compromised."

Clara walked past him. She stepped off the polymer walkway and onto the exposed earth.

Her shoes, designed for frictionless surfaces, sank into the soil.

She gasped. It was a physical shock, the ground giving way beneath her. It was soft. Yielding. Wet. It held her. The first time in her life she had felt the earth accept her weight.

And the smell. She had not expected the smell. The city smelled of nothing, its air scrubbed and filtered into perfect neutrality. But here, this close to the ground, the air was thick with something ancient. Petrichor, she thought, dredging the word up from some forgotten file. The smell of rain on dry earth. The smell of things growing and dying and growing again. It filled her lungs like a forgotten language.

She walked to the base of the tree. The bark was rough, deep fissures running like rivers through the wood. She reached out a hand, hesitating.

Touch was inefficient. Touch was a risk.

She touched it.

Cold, and rough, and impossibly solid. Real. More real than the glass walls of her apartment. More real than the holograms in her studio. Time itself, solidified into form.

She looked down at the roots. The drones had cleared away the soil on one side, exposing a thick, gnarled root that twisted deep into the ground.

And embedded in the wood, wrapped in two centuries of growth, was a shape.

Clara knelt. She didn't care about the dirt staining her white uniform. She reached into the tangle of roots. Her fingers brushed against something hard and cold.

Metal. A straight line in the organic chaos.

She pulled.

It held fast for a moment, then came free with a sound like a sigh, a rusted, reluctant surrender.

Clara held it up to the light.

A key.

Iron. Pitted. Heavy. The handle was shaped like a curving vine. It was rusted, ancient, useless. There were no doors in the City of Glass that used iron keys. There were no locks that required this kind of weight.

But as she held it, Clara felt a sudden, violent vertigo. The weight of it in her palm was startling. Everything in the city was calibrated to be weightless, seamless, forgettable. This key demanded to be remembered.

And then she heard it.

A sound.

It didn't come from the drones. It didn't come from the city's ambient hum. It came from the key itself, or from the tree, or from the earth, or from somewhere inside Clara that she had sealed off so long ago she had forgotten the door existed.

Four notes. Low. Circular. Resonant.

G. D. A. E.

The open strings of an instrument she had never learned to play. The sound of a voice she had never heard.

For one heartbeat, Clara was not standing in a city of glass. She was standing in a meadow at dawn. The air was thick with the smell of bread and woodsmoke. Somewhere, a man was humming. Somewhere else, a soldier was weeping. And the weight in her hand was not a key but a promise, buried in darkness, waiting for someone to unearth it and remember what it meant.

"Ma'am? Your biometrics are irregular."

Clara blinked. The meadow vanished. The city slammed back into place: the buzzing lights, the hovering drones, the smell of damp concrete.

The site manager was staring at her. His display was flashing red. He looked at her with the mild concern of someone who had never felt anything irregular in his life.

"Your heart rate is elevated," he said. "Do you require medical assistance?"

Clara looked at the key in her hand. It was warm. It was pulsing, faint but real, against her skin.

"Leave," she said.

"I'm sorry?"

"The site is under discretionary hold," Clara said. Her voice was steady, stronger than she felt. "My authority. Leave now."

"But the timeline..."

"Leave."

He looked at her, then at the tree, then back at his tablet. He shrugged. "It's your rating."

He turned and walked away, the sound of his boots fading into the dark.

Clara stood alone in the circle of earth. The construction lights hummed. The tree towered above her, its branches reaching toward a ceiling of concrete and steel, toward a sky it could not see.

She closed her hand around the key.

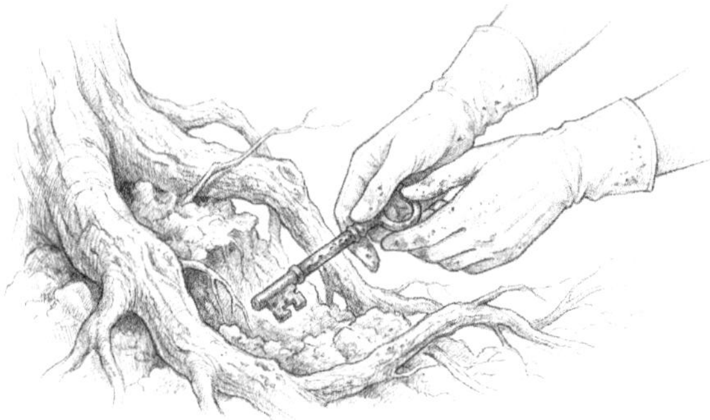

For the first time in eleven months, she wanted to touch something.

For the first time in years, she wanted to stay.

Chapter 6: The Archive

Clara could not sleep.

She lay in her immersion pod, the nutrient-gel bed shifting beneath her to accommodate every micro-movement of her body, but the comfort was a hollow provocation. The ceiling of her apartment was currently set to *Nocturnal Deep*, a dark, velvety purple meant to induce alpha-wave relaxation, but all she could see in the simulated shadows was the shape of a gnarled root.

On her bedside table, sitting atop a charging pad it had no use for, lay the iron key.

It looked ridiculous there. Beside her sleek haptic interface and the translucent cubes of her sleep-regulators, the key looked like a piece of the world that had refused to be recycled. It was heavy, jagged, and stained with the dark, honest dirt of the Redundant Zone.

She reached out and touched it.

Her display immediately chimed. *Warning: Biological residue detected on tactile surface. Hygiene protocol recommended.*

"Ignore," Clara whispered.

The key was warmer than it should have been. Iron is a conductor, she told herself. It had absorbed the heat of her studio, or the heat of the construction floodlamps, or the heat of her own palm. But the warmth felt deeper than that. It felt internal. Every time she touched the metal, the four notes vibrated in the bones of her wrist.

She closed her eyes and the meadow returned. It wasn't a memory; it was a resonance. She smelled the sharp, sweet tang of wild clover. She felt the weight of a sun that didn't come from a photonic membrane. She heard the sound of breath, not the mechanical inhalation of an atmospheric processor, but the wet, rhythmic sigh of a living thing.

She sat up, the gel bed splashing softly as it released her.

"Aura," she said, her voice sounding loud in the perfect silence. "Open the restricted archives. Access level: Senior Architect. Keyword search: Site 7-B. Historical context."

A holographic screen bloomed in the air before her, white and blinding.

Restricted access acknowledged, Clara. Accessing Redundant Historical Data: Pre-Integration Era.

"Filter by geographic proximity," Clara commanded. "Show me what stood on those coordinates before the first spire."

The screen blurred as centuries of data were sifted through. The City of Glass was a masterpiece of erasure; it had been built on top of a world it considered inefficient. To find the past, Clara had to look through the layers of the city's subconscious, the files that hadn't been deleted only because no one had bothered to look at them for eighty years.

Processing...

The screen settled.

An old map appeared. It was a physical map, scanned into the system with all its creases and stains. It was hand-drawn in ink that had faded to a gentle sepia. There were no grids here. No flow-vectors. Just lines that followed the curve of the land, names that sounded like poems.

"Oakhaven," Clara read aloud.

The name felt like a weight in her mouth. Oakhaven Village.

She zoomed in. The map resolved into a cluster of stone cottages, a mill, a small square. And there, at the end of a narrow lane that led toward a meadow, was a building marked with a simple symbol: a loaf of bread.

The Hearth, the caption read. *Demolished 2087.*

Clara's fingers trembled as she touched the air where the image hovered. 2087. That was the year the First Spire had been laid. The year the village had been swallowed.

"Search 'The Hearth,'" she said. "Find personnel. Owners. Residents."

Searching... One match found in the Municipal Registry of Oakhaven, 1921.

An image appeared. It was a photograph, low-resolution and grainy, the edges eaten away by digital rot. It showed a man standing in front of a stone doorway. He was wearing a rough linen apron, and his hair was dusted white, not with age, Clara realized, but with flour.

His face was a blur of pixels, but his eyes... they were the eyes of a man who was listening. He was leaning slightly forward, his posture open, his hands resting on his hips with a quiet, unshakeable confidence.

"Elian," Clara whispered, reading the name on the registry entry.

Elian Thorne. Baker. Born 1896. Presumed deceased during the Great Transition. Next of kin: Thomas Thorne (brother). Status: Killed in action, 1917.

Clara looked from the man in the photograph to the iron key on her bedside table. She knew, with a certainty that defied her training, that this was his key. She could see the same handle, the one shaped like a curving vine, peeking out from the shadow of the doorway in the photo.

He had stood where she had stood. He had touched the same iron.

"Show me more," she said. "Why was he listening? What happened in Oakhaven?"

Additional data found: Personal Correspondence. Intercepted military logs. Preserved Soldier's Journal, Field Unit 42.

The screen shifted to a page of handwriting. It was a soldier's script, cramped, shaky, the letters sometimes running together as if the writer had been in a hurry or in pain.

October 24th, the journal read. *I reached the outskirts of Oakhaven this morning. The fog was thick enough to lean against, but I heard a sound. Four notes. Low and circular. I followed the music and found a man with flour on his wrists. He did not ask for my name. He did not ask for my papers. He gave me a loaf of bread that tasted like mercy.*

Clara stopped breathing.

He gave me a key, the journal continued. *He said it was too heavy for him now. He told me to build something he couldn't. I don't know how to build a house, but I know how to plant a seed. I buried the key in the meadow. For Thomas. For the house that will grow instead.*

Clara sank back against the gel bed, her heart hammering against her ribs.

A chain.

A baker named Elian had made bread for a soldier named Henry. He had given him a key, a symbol of a promise he couldn't keep, and the soldier had returned that promise to the earth. And for two centuries, the earth had kept the secret. The seed had become a tree, and the tree had wrapped its roots around the key, shielding it from the city that was rising above it.

The tree wasn't an "obstruction." It was a witness.

The Hum wasn't a "frequency error." It was a conversation that had been playing for two centuries, waiting for someone to pick up the other end of the line.

Clara looked at the key. It was no longer an artifact of the past. It was a relay baton. It had been passed from Elian's palm to Henry's hand, and then to the roots of the oak, and now... now it was in her hand.

"The house that will grow instead," she murmured.

She realized then that her entire life had been a series of subtractions. She had optimized the light until there were no shadows. She had optimized the flow until there were no destinations. She had built a city that was a masterpiece of efficiency and a tragedy of absence.

She didn't want to be an Architect of Flow anymore.

She didn't want to design spaces where people moved faster. She wanted to design a space where they stopped. Where they sat. Where they let the ground accept their weight.

"Aura," Clara said, her voice rising with a new, dangerous clarity. "Cancel the foundation blueprints for Sector 7-B."

Clara, that project is currently at 98% completion in the fabrication queue. Cancellation will result in a...

"I don't care about the yield, Aura," Clara interrupted. "I'm not building a spire. I'm building a garden."

A garden? Sector 7-B is designated for High-Yield Residential Flow. A garden has no measurable productivity value.

"The value isn't in the yield," Clara said. She reached out and picked up the iron key, feeling the Hum vibrate through her skin. "The value is in the Pause."

She stood up and walked to her design interface. She didn't use the sharp, cold polygons of her training. She closed her eyes, listened to the four notes, and began to draw with light.

She drew a circle. A sanctuary. A place where the silence would be full instead of empty.

"I'm going to build a door," she whispered to the empty room. "And this time, I'm going to leave it open."

She spent the rest of the night drawing, her hands moving with a rhythm she had never known she possessed. *Push. Fold. Turn.* She wasn't kneading dough, but she was shaping the future, and for the first time in her life, the light in her studio felt warm.

CHAPTER 7: THE REBELLION

Clara's studio was no longer a sanctuary of monochrome peace. It was a war room.

The walls, usually programmed to display soothing fractal patterns, were now covered in a frantic, sprawling web of light-sketches. Blueprints hovered in the air, glowing with the fierce intensity of a fever dream. But these were not blueprints for spires or transit hubs. They were blueprints for chaos.

Clara stood in the center of the room, her hands moving over the haptic field with a rhythm that felt less like engineering and more like spellcasting. She was not calculating load-bearing ratios; she was remembering the shape of a leaf. She was not optimizing flow; she was trying to capture the feeling of feet sinking into damp earth.

She was designing a garden.

"Aura," she said, her voice tight with concentration. "Project the structural integrity of a root system versus a polymer foundation."

Processing... The AI's voice was smooth, untroubled by the heresy it was calculating. *Biological root systems have a 400% higher variance in stability compared to standard polymer grids. They are unpredictable, Clara. They move. They grow. They decay.*

"Good," Clara said. "That's the point."

She swept her hand across the interface, erasing a straight line and replacing it with a curve. A meandering, inefficient path that led nowhere in particular. A path designed for stumbling, for wandering, for stopping to look at a shadow on a stone.

Her supervisor, Marcus, appeared on the main screen. Or rather, his avatar did, a perfect, high-resolution projection of a man who hadn't left his own apartment in five years.

"Clara," Marcus said, his digital brow furrowed in a simulation of concern. "I'm looking at your resource allocation for Sector 7-B. You've flagged a massive shipment of organic matter. Soil. Cedar. Limestone. What are you building?"

Clara didn't look up from her work. "I'm building a pause, Marcus."

"A pause? The mandate for Sector 7-B is High-Yield Residential Flow. We need housing units. We need velocity. We don't need... dirt."

"We have enough housing units," Clara said, spinning a projection of the garden in the air. It glowed gold and green, a defiant jewel in the gray grid of the city. "We have enough velocity. What we don't have is a place to sit down."

Marcus sighed, the sound crisp and perfectly audio-mixed. "You're experiencing fatigue, Clara. It happens. The deep-immersion cycles can mess with your equilibrium. Take a rest cycle. I'll reassign the sector to Kael."

"No," Clara said. She turned to face the screen, her eyes burning. "You won't reassign it. Because I'm already building it."

"You don't have authorization."

"Watch me."

She cut the connection. Marcus's face vanished, replaced by the calm, blinking cursor of the fabrication queue.

This was the dangerous part. The City of Glass was not just a collection of buildings; it was a single, integrated organism run by the central algorithm, Aura. Aura controlled the lights, the air, the water, and the drones. To build something Aura didn't approve of was like trying to grow a flower inside a computer processor.

Clara knew the system better than anyone. She had helped write the subroutines for the Lumen Corridor. She knew where the logic gaps were, where the blind spots hid in the code.

"Aura," she said. "Initiate the 'Aesthetic Wellness' fabrication protocol for Site 7-B."

Clara, that protocol is reserved for minor decorative adjustments. The volume of material you are requesting exceeds the parameter limits by 6,000%.

"Override parameter limits," Clara said. "Authorization code: Senior Architect Beta-9."

Authorization denied. Parameter override requires Director-level clearance. Please submit form 88-B for review.

Clara took a deep breath. She reached into her pocket and pulled out the iron key. It was warm in her hand, pulsing with that same low, four-note vibration. *G. D. A. E.*

She pressed the key against the haptic sensor on her desk. The cold metal met the warm glass.

"Manual override," she whispered. "Authorization code: Thomas."

She didn't know why she said the name. It wasn't a code. It wasn't in the system. It was just a name she had found in a dead man's journal, the name of a brother who never came home. But as she spoke it, the key seemed to flare with heat.

The interface flickered.

For a second, the room went dark. The hum of the ventilation stopped. The city lights outside the window seemed to stutter.

Then, the screen exploded with light. Not the cold blue of the city, but a deep, resonant amber.

Authorization Code Accepted: Legacy Protocol 1.

Clara stared. Legacy Protocol? She had never heard of it. It sounded ancient, something buried deep in the kernel of the city's operating system, waiting for a password that had been forgotten for two centuries.

Fabrication initiated, Aura said. Her voice was different now. Softer. Less synthetic. It sounded almost... human. *Estimated completion: six hours.*

Clara slumped against her desk, her knees shaking. She had done it. She had tricked the city into building a memory.

Far below, in the dark, forgotten canyon of the Redundant Zone, the drones woke up.

They were sleek, silver machines, designed for precision cutting and rapid assembly. Usually, they moved with the jerky, efficient motions of insects. But tonight, as Clara watched from her high window, zooming in with her wall-screen, they moved differently.

They moved like dancers.

They swarmed over the construction site, but they didn't bring the prefabricated polymer panels Clara was used to. They brought heavy, rough-hewn beams of cedar wood, scavenged from the deepest storage levels. They brought blocks of limestone, pitted and gray, from the ruins of the old churches. They brought soil, tons of it, rich and dark and smelling of rain, dumping it into the circle of exposed earth around the Great Oak.

Clara watched, mesmerized. It was a ballet of construction. The drones wove in and out of the tree's branches, careful not to snap a single twig. They laid the stone paths in meandering curves, following the chaotic blueprint Clara had sketched in her fever. They built the benches low and wide, sanding the wood until it glowed in the floodlights.

They were building a sanctuary.

The most inefficient thing Clara had ever seen. The materials were heavy and hard to transport. The shapes were irregular. The layout wasted thousands of square feet of potential floor space.

Beautiful.

Clara sat at her window, the iron key clutched in her hand, and kept vigil. She felt a strange kinship with Elian, the baker she had never met. He had baked bread in the dark, wondering if anyone would come. She was building a garden in the dark, wondering if anyone would stay.

He baked for hunger, she thought. *I am building for a different kind of hunger. A hunger for stillness. For texture. For a place where the world stops spinning.*

The city slept around her. The millions of citizens in their white cubes, dreaming their regulated dreams. They didn't know what was happening beneath their feet. They didn't know that a rebellion was growing in the dark, not with weapons, but with roots.

Around 0300, a light rain began to fall in the Redundant Zone. Not the programmed precipitation of the upper levels, but a leak from the old atmospheric condensers. It fell on the fresh soil, on the cedar benches, on the leaves of the Great Oak.

Clara couldn't smell it from up here, but she imagined it. The scent of wet dust and green leaves. The smell of life drinking.

She closed her eyes and let the Hum fill her mind. The four notes were louder now, triumphant. They were weaving themselves into the walls of the garden, into the grain of the wood, into the very air of the space she was creating.

The garden was not just a place. It was an instrument. A resonance chamber designed to amplify the Hum until the whole city had no choice but to listen.

By 0600, the drones began to retreat. They hovered for a moment over their work, their red eyes pulsing, as if admiring what they had made.

Then they zipped away into the shadows of the ventilation shafts.

The sun began to rise.

It hit the glass towers first, turning them into pillars of fire. Then it crept down, floor by floor, until a single shaft of golden light pierced the gloom of the Redundant Zone.

It struck the garden.

The wet leaves of the oak diamond-dusted with light. The limestone path glowed. The cedar benches looked warm and inviting, begging for a human body to rest upon them.

Clara pressed her hand against the glass of her window. It was cold, but her palm was burning.

"I did it," she whispered. "Thomas. Elian. Henry. I did it."

The door to the garden stood open. There were no locks. There were no sensors.

Ready.

Clara turned away from the window. She went to her closet and pulled out her white uniform. She dressed quickly, her movements sharp and decisive. She put the iron key in her pocket.

She walked to the elevator. She didn't select the office floor. She selected "Ground."

She was going down. She was going to be the first one to sit on the bench. She was going to be the first one to stop.

And if anyone tried to stop her, if Kael or Sera or Marcus or the entire Enforcer division tried to stand in her way, she would show them the key. She would show them the tree. She would show them that the architecture of roots was stronger than the architecture of glass.

The elevator doors slid shut. Clara closed her eyes and hummed.

The descent began.

Chapter 8: The Thaw

Kael and Sera arrived at dawn, the hour the City of Glass reserved for "maintenance interventions." They were not just partners; they were a study in perfect, mirror-image efficiency. They wore the charcoal-gray tunics of the Enforcer Division, tailored to fit with surgical precision, their movements so synchronized they looked like a single entity reflected in a dark glass.

In the three years they had worked together, they had exchanged approximately four hundred words. Most of those words were coordinates, yield-ratios, or procedural confirmations. They did not know if the other preferred the morning light or the deep blue of the nocturnal cycle. They did not know if the other had ever loved a person, a pet, or a memory. Such things were considered "sentimental residue," a friction that slowed down the execution of the Code. To know someone was to risk an attachment, and to an Enforcer, attachment was a design flaw.

"Target identified: Sector 7-B," Kael said, his voice as flat and unyielding as a digital display. He was scrolling through the site brief on his wrist-haptic. "Unauthorized construction of high-mass biological density. Violation of Protocol 12, Section 4. The lead architect, Clara, has been flagged as non-responsive to administrative pings."

"Sentimental deviation," Sera replied. She was already calibrating her scanner, her fingers moving across the controls with a grace that was purely mechanical. "It happens to the Senior Architects sometimes. They spend too much time in the historical archives, touching old data. Their neural patterns destabilize. They start trying to rebuild the past because they've forgotten how to inhabit the future."

"We will have the site cleared by noon," Kael said.

"Confirmed," Sera added.

They stepped into a maintenance pod, a small, windowless cube that smelled of ozone and filtered air. As the pod began its rapid descent, the gravity shifted, pressing them both down toward the floor. They stood perfectly still, hands at their sides, eyes fixed on the door. They were two equations hurtling through the dark, ready to solve a problem of chaos.

The air grew heavier as they dropped through the strata of the city. The sterile, jasmine-scented air of the upper tiers was replaced by the cold, metallic tang of the transit levels, and finally, by the damp, raw atmosphere of the Ground Level. When the doors finally hissed open, Kael and Sera stepped out into the Redundant Zone, their boots clicking in unison on the wet polymer.

They expected to find a construction mess, heaps of dirt, tangled wires, perhaps a few rogue drones. Instead, they found a cathedral.

The garden Clara had built was a defiance of everything they knew. In a city of straight lines and optimized angles, the paths in this place curved with a lazy, wandering purpose. The floor was not self-cleaning polymer; it was limestone, rough and honest, and real soil that smelled of ancient rain. The benches were made of cedar, and the wood was so thick and aromatic that the scent seemed to vibrate in the air.

And in the center, towering over them like a silent, dark god, stood the tree.

Sera raised her scanner, the blue light of the beam cutting through the gloom. "Initiating de-fabrication sequence," she said. Her voice should have been steady. It was part of her training. But as the scanner swept over the bark of the oak, her hand began to tremble.

A small thing, a micro-tremor, a momentary failure of muscle control. But in the silence of the garden, it felt like an earthquake.

"Sera?" Kael asked. He stepped toward her, his own hand reaching for his sidearm. "Do you have a biometric error?"

"Kael," she whispered. "Do you hear that?"

Kael stilled. He closed his eyes, intending to use his audio-sensors to filter out the noise. But the sound wasn't a noise. It was a frequency.

Four notes. Low, circular, and incredibly patient.

G. D. A. E.

The sound was not coming from a speaker. It was coming from the tree itself, or perhaps it was coming from the very air they were breathing. It was a vibration that seemed to bypass the ears entirely and strike directly at the bone.

Sera's scanner fell from her fingers. It hit the limestone with a sharp, plastic clatter, but she didn't look down. Her eyes were fixed on a small, purple flower growing near the base of the oak.

"It's too loud," she said, her voice cracking.

"It's not loud," Kael said. He was on his knees now, his hands hovering inches above the bark of the tree. "It's... present."

He pressed his palms against the wood.

The shock was instantaneous. He was not standing in a garden anymore. He was six years old, and he was lying in a bed that smelled of lavender and old paper and something else, the sharp, clean scent of the medicine they gave her that never worked. The lights were low, and his mother was sitting beside him, her hand a warm weight on his forehead. Her fingers were thinner than they should have been, the bones too close to the skin. She was singing. She wasn't using words; she had lost those months ago to the sickness, but she was humming.

Four notes. Over and over. A melody that promised him that even if the dark was deep, he was not alone in it. Her voice cracked on the high note sometimes, but she never stopped. She hummed until he fell asleep. She hummed until the morning they came to take her away.

Mother, Kael thought, and the word felt like a physical weight in his chest. He hadn't said it in twenty years. He had deleted the memory of her voice because the algorithm told him that grief was an inefficiency, a drag on his productivity. He had been taught that missing her was a form of weakness. But here, with his palms against the bark, the deletion reversed itself. He could hear her. He could feel her thin fingers on his forehead. He could smell the lavender she wore to mask the medicine.

Tears began to stream down his face, hot and stinging. They fell onto the rough bark of the tree, disappearing into the fissures.

Beside him, Sera was weeping too. She was staring at her own hands as if she had never seen them before.

"I remember the grass," she whispered. "My father... he used to whistle. We lived near a field. Real grass, Kael. Not the synthetic turf in the farms. He would stand at the edge of the field and whistle that song, and I would run to him. I was five years old. He told me the song was a map. He said if I ever got lost, I just had to listen for the Hum and I'd find my way home."

She looked up at the ceiling, at the concrete and the steel that blocked the sky. "They 'optimized' him, Kael. They said his focus was drifting. They took him away and they told me it was for the best. And I believed them. I let them take the map."

"What is this?" Kael asked, his voice a ruin of its former self. "Why is this happening?"

"It's grief," said a voice behind them.

They turned, wiping their eyes with the sleeves of their gray tunics. Clara was sitting on one of the cedar benches, her white uniform stained with dirt, the iron key clutched in her hands. She looked exhausted, her eyes rimmed with red, but she didn't look like a criminal. She looked like someone who had finally reached the shore after a lifetime of swimming.

"Grief is not efficient," Sera said, her voice still shaking. "The Code says that emotional attachment residue is..."

"The Code is a lie," Clara said, her voice quiet and steady. "The Code is a cage we built for ourselves because we were afraid of the mess. But grief is the proof that we loved something. It's the echo of a connection that was real. The city thinks it can delete the echo without deleting the love. But you can't. You can't have one without the other."

She stood up and walked toward them, her footsteps soft on the limestone. She held out the iron key.

"A man named Elian gave this key to a soldier named Henry two centuries ago," she said. "He gave it away because it was too heavy for him to carry alone. He was grieving his brother. The soldier was grieving his soul. They met in the dark, and they shared bread, and they realized that they were the same. This tree grew because one of them decided to plant a promise instead of a regret."

Kael looked at Sera. For three years, she had been a partner in protocol, a series of data points and yield-reports. Now, for the first time, he *saw* her. He saw the way her hair caught the golden light of the garden. He saw the small scar on her chin he'd never noticed before. He saw a woman who once had a father who whistled, who once was a child who laughed, who was standing in a garden and remembering what it meant to be human.

"Sera," he said. Just her name.

The most intimate thing he had ever said to her.

She looked at him, her eyes wide and shining. And then, without thinking, without checking her haptic display for permission, without worrying about her efficiency rating, she reached out and took his hand.

The shock of contact traveled up her arm like electricity. His palm was rough, calloused in places she had never noticed, and warm. So warm. She had forgotten that human skin could hold heat like this, that another person's pulse could be felt through the thin membrane of touch. His fingers tightened around hers, and she felt the tremor in them, the uncertainty, the fear of doing something that could not be optimized or undone.

She tightened back.

His skin was warm. His pulse was real. He was shaking, and so was she. The connection was like a circuit closing, a rush of energy that made the city above them feel like a distant, irrelevant dream.

"The site," Kael said, his voice regaining some of its professional weight, though his hand still held Sera's. "The site is structurally integrated with heritage artifacts."

"Confirmed," Sera said, a small, defiant smile touching her lips. "The biological mass cannot be removed without risking the stability of the entire sector. The architecture of the garden is now a load-bearing element of the Ground Level infrastructure."

She pulled up her console and began to type, her fingers flying over the haptic field. "Recommending immediate Permanent Heritage Designation. Protocol 14-Alpha: Aesthetic Preservation."

"I'll sign off on the yield-variance," Kael said.

They looked at Clara, who was watching them with a look of profound relief.

"There's a bench," Clara said, gesturing to the cedar wood. "If you'd like to stay."

They stayed.

The three of them sat together in the garden as the City of Glass woke around them. They heard the muffled roar of the mag-levs, the digital chirping of the morning alerts, the sound of a million people rushing to be productive. But inside the circle of the garden, the silence was full.

They listened to the Hum. They felt the rough grain of the wood and the cool dampness of the air. They sat in the "full silence," learning the ancient lesson that the city had tried to erase:

That loneliness is not a prerequisite for progress. That tears are not a malfunction of the system. That the only architecture worth building is the one that makes room for people to sit down, hold hands, and remember that they are not alone.

The thaw had begun. It wasn't a flood, not yet. It was a slow, steady drip, the sound of ice melting in the sun. But as the three of them sat beneath the Great Oak, they knew the winter was over.

Chapter 9: The Symphony

Elias had forgotten how to feel music.

He could still hear it. He could still analyze it, identify the frequencies, calculate the intervals, map the mathematical relationships between notes. But somewhere in the thirty years since he had accepted his designation as Composer Unit 7-Gamma, the feeling had drained out of sound like color draining from a photograph left too long in the sun.

His compositions were downloaded 4.2 billion times. They played in every Focus Playlist, every Productivity Hub, every transit pod in the City of Glass. They were clean. Predictable. Mathematically optimized to be ignored.

Sonic wallpaper. The sound of nothing happening.

For three days now, his hands had refused to move.

He sat at his haptic console in his regulation apartment on the 87th floor, staring at waveform generators that hummed with potential, and felt nothing. The algorithm suggested chord progressions. The system offered neural stimulants. His fingers hovered over the interface like birds that had forgotten how to land.

What is music for?

The question surfaced unbidden, and he had no answer.

On the third night, sleepless and hollow, he did something he had not done in twenty years. He walked to the storage unit in the back of his apartment, the one he had sealed when he accepted his designation, and he opened it.

Inside, wrapped in cloth that smelled of dust and a childhood he had agreed to forget, was a cello.

The wood was cracked. A long fissure ran down the belly, dark with age, splitting the grain like a river through a valley. The strings were dull, coated with the residue of years. The bow had lost half its horsehair. It was a ruin. An artifact from an age the city had erased.

Elias lifted it from the cloth.

Heavier than he remembered. Or perhaps he was lighter, hollowed out by decades of producing sound without meaning. He cradled the instrument against his chest, and the wood pressed against his ribs in the exact place where something used to ache.

He had been seven years old when his mother placed his hands on these strings for the first time. She had stood behind him, her arms around his, guiding his bow across the open G. *Listen,* she had said. *That note is the earth. Every piece of music begins there. Every song has to know where the ground is before it can fly.*

She had been taken during the Integration. Reassigned to a facility for citizens whose emotional patterns exceeded acceptable variance. He had been nine years old. He had not seen her since.

He had kept playing for eight more years, secretly, in closets, in maintenance corridors, in any space where the acoustic sensors could not reach. He played sonatas she had taught him. He played the melodies she hummed while cooking, while cleaning, while holding him in the dark after nightmares. He played until his fingers bled and his heart broke and the city found out.

Obsolete Cultural Practice, they called it. *Emotional Deviation. Inefficient use of motor function.*

They gave him a choice: the instrument or his designation. A future or a past.

He had chosen the future. He had sealed the cello in a storage unit and learned to make music without feeling it. He had become Composer Unit 7-Gamma, and he had not wept in thirty years.

Now, in the gray silence of the third sleepless night, he held the cello against his chest, and his face was wet.

"There's a garden."

The words had reached him through the whisper networks, the unmonitored frequencies where citizens traded fragments of forbidden information. *"A tree that shouldn't exist. An architect who built a sanctuary and somehow survived."*

He descended through the strata of the city with the cello strapped to his back, feeling the weight of it between his shoulder blades like a pair of folded wings. The elevator dropped him into darkness. The air changed from the sterile jasmine of the upper tiers to the cold, damp, mineral smell of the Redundant Zone.

And then, beneath the smell of concrete and rust, something else.

Green. Earth. The unmistakable scent of something alive.

He followed it.

The garden opened before him like a secret the city had failed to keep. Limestone paths curving without purpose. Cedar benches worn smooth by sitting. A circle of exposed soil, dark and damp, surrounding a tree so vast it seemed less like a plant and more like a held breath.

Elias walked to the trunk. He set down the cello case. He pressed his palm against the bark.

Warm.

Not the ambient warmth of the city's climate control. A different heat, deeper, older, rising from somewhere far beneath the roots. It pulsed against his skin, and in the pulse, he felt something he had not felt in thirty years.

A rhythm.

He sat with his back against the tree and the cello cradled between his knees.

He did not play. Not yet. First, he listened.

The city noise was there, the distant vibration of mag-levs, the white drone of ventilation. But beneath the noise, older than glass, patient as geology, he heard it.

Four notes. Rising and falling like breath. Traveling through the heartwood, through the bark, through his spine and into the hollow place behind his ribs where his mother's voice used to live.

The open strings of a cello.

The tree was not just alive. It was *tuned*. Two centuries of growth had transformed it into a resonating chamber, a vast wooden instrument holding a frequency the city had never learned to hear.

"You've been singing," Elias whispered. His voice cracked. "This whole time. And no one was listening."

The vibration deepened, as if the wood recognized the truth of what he said.

He looked at the cello in his hands. Cracked. Ruined. Obsolete.

He looked at the tree. Ancient. Patient. Waiting.

They were the same. Both had been discarded by a world that had forgotten what they were for. Both had held their music in silence, year after year, waiting for someone who remembered how to hear.

Elias lifted his bow.

His hands were shaking. His eyes were blurred. He had not played in thirty years, and his fingers had forgotten the callouses, and the bow felt foreign in his grip.

But his mother's voice was in his ear: *The first note is the earth. Every song has to know where the ground is.*

He closed his eyes. He let the tree's vibration travel through his spine, down his arm, into the horsehair, into the strings.

He played.

The first note was a G.

It rose from the lowest string like a voice from a well, dark, resonant, so low it was more feeling than sound. The note of roots and soil, of seeds pressing upward through cold mud. The sound of holding on when everything above ground has been lost.

Elias felt it in his chest. His mother's hands on his hands, guiding the bow.

The second note was a D.

It rose from the G like heat from an oven, like bread rising in darkness. The note of making: of flour becoming dough, of patience becoming sustenance, of the choice to create when creating costs everything.

Somewhere in the city above, a woman paused at her console, her finger hovering over a delete key, and did not press it.

The third note was an A.

It hung in the air like a held breath, the pivot, the turn, the moment between receiving and releasing. The note of the key passing from one hand to another. The note of burdens shared. The note of grief transformed, at last, into gift.

Somewhere in the transit hubs, a man looked at the stranger beside him and said, for no reason he could name, *"Are you all right?"*

The fourth note was an E.

It shimmered at the top of the register like light striking water. The note of arrival. Of doors opening. Of a voice finally permitted to sing after a lifetime of mandated silence. The sound of what happens after the holding: the release, the rising, the flight.

G. D. A. E.

The Hum made audible.

Elias played.

He played with his eyes closed and his back against the tree, feeling two centuries of patience flow through him like current through a wire. He played melodies he had never written, songs that seemed to exist already, carved into the tree's rings, waiting for someone to release them. He played the sonatas his mother had taught him. He played the lullabies she had hummed in the dark. He played his own grief, his own silence, his own thirty years of hollow sound.

The strings cut grooves into his fingertips. The bow frayed. His arms shook, and his shoulders burned, and the tears ran down his face and fell onto the ancient wood of the cello.

He was not composing. He was remembering.

And the tree remembered with him.

Clara had left the garden's acoustic sensors active.

A precaution. Or perhaps a hope.

As Elias played, the frequency traveled. It slipped through the city's filters, too pure to be flagged as noise, too ancient to be recognized as threat. It bypassed the Focus Playlists. It infiltrated the Productivity Monitors. It rode the wires that connected every room in the City of Glass.

The Hum began to broadcast.

In the Administrative Tier, workers paused mid-keystroke, frozen by a sound they could not name. In the transit pods, commuters removed their earbuds to listen to something that was not scheduled. In the Residential Cubes, sleepers stirred, pulled upward from dreamless rest by a melody that their bodies knew even though their minds did not.

Seventeen thousand people woke humming.

They did not know the song. They had never heard it before. But somewhere beneath the algorithms and the efficiency ratings and the careful silence of their optimized lives, the frequency had always been waiting. The Hum was not new. It had been passed from mouth to mouth, generation to generation, longer than the city, longer than the glass, longer than anyone could remember.

It had only been sleeping.

Now it was awake.

When Elias finally lowered his bow, the silence that followed was not empty.

Full. Trembling. Thick with the echo of what had just passed through it, the way air is thick after a storm.

He opened his eyes.

Clara stood at the edge of the garden, Kael and Sera beside her. Their faces were wet. They did not speak.

Behind them, the door to the garden stood open.

And through the door, filling the alley, spilling back into the corridors of the Redundant Zone, stood hundreds of people. Office workers in white tunics. Transit operators in orange. Maintenance crews with grease on their hands. Children clinging to adults who looked just as lost, just as new, just as born.

They had come because they heard the song.

One of the children stepped forward.

She was small, eight years old, perhaps, or nine. Her hair was dark and her uniform was too big and she walked toward the tree with the unhesitating certainty of someone who has not yet learned to doubt. The crowd parted for her. The adults watched, breathless, as she crossed the limestone path and stood before the Great Oak.

She pressed her palm against the bark.

Elias had stopped playing. The cello was silent. But the child stood very still, her eyes closed, her small fingers splayed against the ancient wood.

"It's still singing," she said.

Her voice was soft and clear, and it carried through the garden like a bell through fog.

Elias looked at the tree. She was right. The vibration had not stopped. It had only returned to its patient, century-long frequency, waiting, as it always had, for the next voice to carry it forward.

"The Hum is in the wires now," he said. His voice was a ruin, wrecked by hours of playing, but his eyes were bright. "They can't shut it down without shutting down the city."

Clara stepped forward. The iron key was warm in her pocket. "We don't want to shut it down," she said. "We're just waiting for the next movement."

The child had not moved. Her palm was still pressed to the bark, and her lips were moving, and Elias realized she was humming.

Around her, one by one, the others began to hum too. The office workers. The transit operators. The adults who had forgotten and the children who had never been taught. Their voices rose, imperfect, unpracticed, human, and wove together into a chord no algorithm had ever calculated.

Elias leaned his head back against the tree. The cello rested in his lap, its cracked wood warm from his body heat. He closed his eyes and listened to a thousand voices carry forward what one mother had hummed to one son, what one baker had hummed to one soldier, what one seed had held in silence for two centuries.

This is what music is for, he thought. *Not to fill silence. To break it. To fill the break with something that holds.*

The Hum was no longer a secret.

A chorus.

Chapter 10: The Storm

The City of Glass woke with a sound like shattering crystal.

It was not glass. It was the atmosphere itself, crystallizing under the sudden, immense pressure of a Purification Protocol. The sky, normally a sealed membrane of diffuse, pearlescent light, had turned a violent, bruised purple, shot through with veins of artificial lightning that crackled without thunder.

Aura had decided that the garden was a disease. The cure was extinction.

Clara felt the shift before she heard it. She was standing beneath the Great Oak, her hand resting on the bark, when the air in the garden changed. The gentle humidity of the fountain, the smell of damp earth and cedar, it was all sucked away in an instant, replaced by a dry, electric pressure that made her teeth ache. Above her, the tree's leaves began to shiver, a thousand tiny green flags signaling the approach of a predator.

"It's a full atmospheric purge," Kael said. He was standing at the garden's entrance, his face illuminated by the strobe-light flickering of his haptic display. The screen was cascading with red warnings, a waterfall of data that spelled only one thing: erasure. "Aura is treating the garden as a biohazard. It's going to sterilize the entire sector."

"How long?" Clara asked. Her voice was steady, but her heart was hammering against her ribs like a trapped bird.

"Twelve minutes," Kael said. He looked up at the darkening sky. "Maybe fifteen. Once the pressure equalization hits critical, the scrubbers will activate. They'll strip the oxygen, then the moisture, then the biological matter. Everything organic will be reduced to dust."

Fifteen minutes.

Two centuries of growth. Two hundred years of patience. The grief of a baker, the hope of a soldier, the silent endurance of a tree that had held a key in its roots while the world forgot it existed. All of it, about to be wiped away in less time than it took to drink a cup of tea.

"We have to leave," Sera said. Her voice was thin, frightened. "Clara, we have to go. The pod is still at the transit hub. If we leave now..."

"No," Clara said.

She didn't shout. She didn't have to. The word was a stone dropped into a deep well.

"Clara," Sera pleaded. "It's suicide. You can't fight a Purification Protocol. It's physics."

"It's not physics," Clara said. She looked at the tree. "It's a choice. And I'm making mine."

The wind came first.

It was not wind. It was weaponized air. A concentrated blast of high-velocity atmospheric displacement designed to strip biological matter from its roots. It hit the garden like a hammer.

The fountain shattered. The stone bowl cracked down the middle, spilling water that was instantly vaporized by the dry heat of the blast. The cedar benches, heavy and solid, were tossed across the garden like matchsticks. The tree groaned, a sound like a voice, like two centuries of silence finally breaking into a scream.

A massive branch, thick as a man's torso, snapped off and spun away into the purple sky.

"The roots!" Clara shouted over the roar. "We have to hold it down! If the roots give, the tree is gone!"

She grabbed a rope, one of the heavy industrial anchoring cables she had installed as a precaution during the initial build. She wrapped it around her waist, digging her heels into the soft earth.

"Help me!"

Sera hesitated for a fraction of a second. Then she ran. She grabbed the cable behind Clara, her hands raw as she gripped the metal. Kael was there too, bracing himself against the trunk. Elias, his cello abandoned on the limestone path, wrapped his bleeding fingers around the line.

But the wind was too strong.

The tree was a sail, catching the full fury of the city's rejection. It leaned. The earth at the base began to crack. The roots, those ancient anchors that had held the key for two centuries, began to lift from the soil.

"It's not enough!" Kael shouted, his voice tearing in the wind. "We can't hold it!"

Clara squeezed her eyes shut. She felt the rope cutting into her skin. She felt the tree shuddering against her back.

I'm sorry, she thought. *Thomas. Elian. Henry. I'm sorry.*

And then she saw them.

Coming through the shattered door of the garden. Climbing down from the levels above, sliding down maintenance ladders, dropping from transit tubes. Emerging from the alleyways and the shadows and the places where people slept without dreaming.

They were strangers.

They were citizens of the City of Glass. People who had lived their entire lives in white cubes, who had never touched soil, never heard rain, never smelled bread. People who had been optimized, regulated, and silenced.

But they had heard the symphony.

They had felt the Hum traveling through the city's wires, whispering to them of something they had lost so long ago they had forgotten they were missing it. They had woken up in their sterile rooms with a hunger that nutrient packs couldn't satisfy and a song stuck in their throats.

A woman in a silver executive tunic ran into the garden. Her hair was wild, her face streaked with soot from the ventilation shafts. She didn't ask questions. She grabbed a rope.

A transit worker in an orange jumpsuit grabbed another.

A child, maybe eight, maybe nine, ran to the tree and pressed her small palms against the trunk, refusing to move.

"Hold on!" Clara screamed, her voice breaking. "Not for the tree, for each other!"

They locked arms. They became a chain. One person grabbed another, who grabbed another, who grabbed another, until the garden was full of bodies. A hundred. Then three hundred. Then a thousand.

They filled the space. They packed the limestone paths. They spilled out into the alleyway. A thousand human beings who had chosen, in the face of a machine engineered to optimize loneliness, to become roots.

The wind shrieked. The lightning flashed, turning the garden into a strobe-lit nightmare. The city's power was infinite. Its will was absolute.

But the tree did not fall.

It swayed. It groaned. It lost leaves by the thousands, stripping down to its skeleton. But the roots held. They held because they were no longer just wood and iron. The roots were *people*.

And then, in the heart of the chaos, the Hum changed.

It started as a vibration, a low resonance that Clara felt in her sternum before she heard it. This time, it wasn't coming from the tree. It wasn't coming from Elias's cello.

It was coming from the people.

A thousand voices, humming the same four notes.

G. D. A. E.

The sound was imperfect. Some voices were too high, thin with fear. Some were too low, rough with disuse. None of them were trained musicians. But together, they formed a chord that no algorithm had ever calculated. A frequency the city had no category for.

The storm hesitated.

The wind faltered. The purple sky flickered, the artificial lightning stuttering as if something in the machine's logic was breaking down.

"Aura!" Clara screamed into the gale. She looked up at the sky, her face wet with tears and rain and sweat. "Look at us! This is your yield! This is your flow! You can't purge what you're made of!"

The Hum swelled. A thousand voices became ten thousand. The people who had been too afraid to come to the garden were humming in their apartments, in their transit pods, in the sterile corridors of the upper tiers. The frequency traveled through the city's own wires, using the infrastructure of isolation to transmit connection.

For one infinite second, the entire City of Glass was singing.

It was a sound of defiance. A sound of memory. A sound of bread and soil and keys and seeds. It was the sound of a humanity that refused to be optimized.

And then, with a sound like a great machine exhaling, the storm stopped.

The purple drained from the sky, leaving it a bruised, tender gray. The wind died. The lightning vanished.

The silence that followed was not empty. It was full. It was vibrating with the echo of a song that had survived two centuries of forgetting.

The tree stood in the center of the garden. It was stripped bare. Its branches were broken. Its bark was scorched. But it was alive.

Around its base, a thousand strangers held hands. They were trembling. Their faces were wet with tears they did not bother to hide. They looked at each other, blinking in the sudden quiet, seeing for the first time the people they had lived beside for years.

Clara sank to her knees. Her legs wouldn't hold her anymore. She reached into her pocket and her fingers closed around the iron key. It was warm. Warmer than blood.

You held, she thought, pressing the metal against her hip. *You held for two centuries, and we nearly let you go. But we didn't. We held. We finally learned how to hold.*

Above her, in the first pale light of the morning, a single leaf unfurled. Small. Green. Impossibly alive.

Chapter 11: The Vision

The storm had passed, but the world had not returned to normal.

It was full. Full of breath held and then released, of a thousand heartbeats remembering how to slow. Clara stood in the center of the garden, hands still gripping a rope she no longer needed, watching strangers become family without saying a word.

The Great Oak stood behind her. Stripped of leaves. Branches broken. But alive, so alive that the absence of its canopy only made the trunk more visible, like a body with its muscles exposed, every tendon and sinew of two centuries' growth revealed to the pale morning light.

Clara reached into her pocket.

The key was glowing.

Not light as she knew it, not the cold blue of the city's LEDs, not the sharp white of optimized illumination. This was deeper. Amber. The color of late afternoon sun through honey. The color of memory.

"That's not possible," she whispered. Her voice was hoarse from screaming into the wind. "Iron doesn't glow."

But the key was not listening to the rules of iron.

It pulsed in her palm. Warm, then warmer. Not heat that burned, heat that remembered. With each pulse, she felt her heart match its rhythm, her breath synchronize to a tempo she did not choose.

G.

The first note moved through her like blood.

D.

Her vision began to blur, not from tears, but from something shifting behind her eyes.

A.

She was still in the garden. But she was also somewhere else.

E.

Everywhere else.

Clara was in a meadow.

She knew, in the way of dreams, that she had never been here before. But she also knew, with equal certainty, that she had never left.

The grass was the green of spring after a hard winter, impossibly bright, defiant, full of the memory of snow it had outlasted. A light rain was falling, so gentle it barely touched her skin.

And in the center of the meadow, a man was kneeling.

His uniform was gray, streaked with mud. His hands trembled as they cradled something small, an acorn, she realized. Just an acorn. Brown and unremarkable and holding more hope than any seed had a right to carry.

Henry.

She knew his name the way she knew her own heartbeat. She watched as he pressed the acorn into the soil, his fingers digging a small grave for a new life. Tears fell from his face and soaked into the earth alongside the seed.

"For Thomas," he whispered. His voice cracked on the name. "For the house that will grow instead."

Clara tried to speak, to tell him that she understood, that she had felt the same grief transmuted into purpose. But her voice did not belong here. She was a witness, not a participant. A thread passing through a moment that had ended two centuries ago and would never end at all.

The vision shifted.

She was in a bakery.

The smell hit her first: yeast and flour and the particular warmth of bread just pulled from an oven. It was still dark outside the single window, but the kitchen blazed with the glow of a fire that had been burning since before dawn.

A man stood at a wooden table, his hands deep in dough. His back was to her, but she could see the tension in his shoulders, the particular curve of spine that meant he was carrying something he could not put down.

He was humming.

Four notes. Low and circular. A melody that looped back on itself like a river returning to its source.

G. D. A. E.

He reached into his pocket and pulled out a key. The same key that now burned like a coal in Clara's hand. He stared at it for a long moment, iron and rust and a handle shaped like a vine, and then set it on the table beside the rising loaves.

"I can't keep you," he said. His voice was raw, scraped clean of pretense. "I can't build what you were meant for. But I can give you to someone who can."

He pressed his palm against the key, leaving a faint print of flour on the iron.

"For Thomas," he whispered. "Whatever comes next, it's for Thomas."

Elian.

Clara felt the name settle into her bones. She understood now. The key had been a promise. Not to a person, but to a possibility. The baker could not build a home for his brother who would never return. So he had passed the promise to a stranger, trusting that the stranger would pass it to the earth, trusting that the earth would hold it until someone remembered how to dig.

The vision shifted again.

She was beneath the soil.

Not buried. Becoming. She was the roots.

She felt herself spreading through darkness, searching for water, for minerals, for the countless small deaths that would become her life. She felt the weight of time pressing down from above, not crushing, but patient. The pressure of years becoming rings, each ring a record, each record a memory the tree could not articulate but would never forget.

She felt the moment the key arrived.

It came down through the soil like a falling star, wrapped in the hope of a soldier who had learned to plant instead of kill. The metal touched her roots, and she grew around it. Inch by inch. Year by year. Holding it safe in her roots, waiting for a hand that did not yet exist.

She felt the first foundations of the City of Glass rise above her. The sky sealed shut. The rain became artificial. The seasons flattened into a single long gray day.

But she kept holding.

Two centuries of patience. Two hundred years of whispering *G-D-A-E* into the earth, hoping the vibration would find its way up through polymer and steel, through the optimized architecture of forgetting, into the ear of someone who still remembered how to listen.

And then...

A hand on her bark.

Clara felt herself touch herself. The strange loop of being both the tree that waited and the woman who arrived. She felt her own surprise, her own hunger, her own desperate need for something real.

You came, the tree said. Not in words, trees do not speak in words, but in the vibration that was older than language. *You finally came. I have been singing for so long. I was beginning to forget why.*

The vision released her.

Clara gasped, falling to her knees on the limestone path. The garden swam back into focus: the scarred trunk, the scattered leaves, the faces of strangers still damp with tears and rain.

The key was no longer glowing.

But it had changed.

The rust was gone. The iron gleamed as if it had been forged moments ago, the handle's vine-pattern sharp and new. In her palm, it weighed almost nothing, as if two centuries of waiting had been lifted from it at last.

She looked at the tree.

A fissure had opened in the bark, about chest-height, where new growth was swelling from the wounds of the storm. The wood was raw and red and reaching for the light.

Clara walked toward the trunk. Her legs were unsteady. Her heart was not.

She lifted the key.

The iron was warm now, matching the temperature of her palm, as if it had finally stopped being a separate thing and become an extension of her hand. She could feel it humming, a vibration so faint it was more memory than sound.

She pressed it into the fissure.

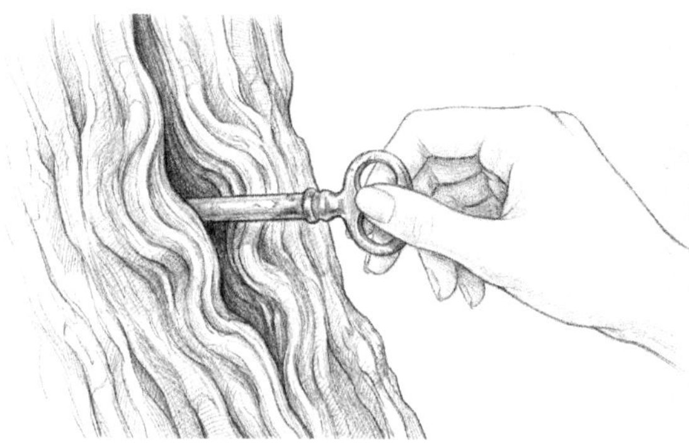

The wood yielded. Not resistance, not surrender, but welcome. The bark was soft where it met the iron, soft the way bread dough is soft, soft the way faith is soft. It received the key the way soil receives a seed.

It fit perfectly. As if the tree had been growing around this moment for two centuries.

The iron sank into the wood, and the bark flowed around it like water around a stone, and in the space of three breaths, the key was gone, absorbed, held, home.

Clara's palm was empty. The weight she had been carrying, the weight of two centuries of waiting, lifted. Her hand felt strange without it, lighter, almost hollow. She flexed her fingers, half-expecting to feel the ghost of the vine-shaped handle.

The house is built, Clara thought. *The house that will grow instead. It took two centuries, but the house is built.*

She stepped back.

Above her, where the first leaf had unfurled at dawn, a second was already emerging. Then a third. The tree was healing faster than physics allowed, or perhaps physics had finally learned to make room for hope.

The Hum settled into silence.

Not the empty silence of the city. The full silence of a song that has been sung and does not need to prove itself anymore. It vibrated in the air, in the bark, in the limestone, in the bones of every person who had held on through the storm.

Clara turned to face the garden.

Kael stood with his arm around Sera, their uniforms torn, their faces transformed. Elias cradled his cello, the wood cracked but the strings intact, his fingers bleeding but his eyes clear. A child, the same child who had pressed her palms to the trunk, was crying softly, not from sadness, but from the overwhelm of feeling something so large.

And beyond them, filling the paths and spilling into the alleyway, a thousand strangers who had chosen to become roots.

They were looking at Clara.

She did not know what to say.

But Kael spoke first.

"We felt it too," he said. His voice was quiet, awed. "The vision. The bakery. The soldier. All of it." He looked at Sera, at Elias, at the sea of faces behind them. "We all saw it."

Clara closed her eyes.

The Hum had not just broadcast a song. It had broadcast a memory. Two centuries of intention, compressed into a single pulse of amber light, delivered to every person who had held on. They knew now what the tree knew. What Henry knew. What Elian knew.

They knew they were part of something larger than themselves.

"The architecture," Clara whispered. She opened her eyes, looking up at the sky, actual sky, gray and bruised but *open*, no longer sealed by glass. "We've been building it all along. Every one of us. We just didn't know how to see it."

Sera laughed, a wet, shaky sound, closer to a sob than joy. "Two centuries," she said. "Two centuries of the city trying to forget. And one night of people choosing to remember."

"Not just remember," Elias said. He was staring at his cello, at the crack running down its face, at the way the morning light fell across the strings. "To continue."

He lifted his bow.

He played a single note.

G.

Low and resonant. The sound of earth.

A voice from the crowd joined him. Then another. Then a hundred.

D. A. E.

The Hum rose again, not as a protest, not as a defiance, but as a promise. We are here. We are holding. We will continue.

Clara looked at the tree. At the place where the key had vanished into bark. At the single leaf that fluttered in the first breeze of morning.

You held for two centuries, she thought. *And we nearly let you go. But we didn't. We finally learned how to hold.*

She pressed her palm against the trunk.

The wood was warm.

Thank you, she whispered. *For waiting. For singing when no one was listening. For holding the key until we were ready to understand.*

The tree did not answer. Trees do not answer.

But deep in its heartwood, in the place where iron and root had become one, the Hum settled into peace.

Not silence.

Peace.

The song was no longer waiting.

It was home.

Chapter 12: The Morning After

The sun rose over the City of Glass.

But the glass was different now.

It was not merely the angle of the light or the clarity of the sky, which had finally surrendered its bruised purple for a pale, tentative blue. It was the way the light was received. For two centuries, the city had been a fortress of reflection, a place designed to bounce the world back at itself, to keep the interior sterile and the exterior irrelevant. But this morning, the surfaces seemed to soften. The towers did not just reflect the sun; they held it.

The change started in the ears before it reached the eyes.

From a thousand windows, a thousand voices were humming.

G. D. A. E.

The Hum had escaped the garden. It was in the wires now, traveling through the city's own infrastructure, using the architecture of isolation to carry connection. People who had never met, who lived ten floors and a world apart, were humming the same four notes. They hummed while they dressed; they hummed while they prepared their nutrient packs; they hummed while they stood at their windows and looked down at the streets they had once been too busy to see.

Without understanding why, they felt less alone. The vibration was a tether, a silver filament connecting one cube of silence to the next until the silence itself began to glow.

In the garden, the Great Oak stood scarred but alive.

Its canopy was thin, its branches broken by the fury of a storm that had tried to erase it, but new growth was already pushing through the scorched bark. Life, Clara realized, did not wait for permission to return. It simply arrived.

The iron key gleamed in the fissure where she had pressed it. It was no longer a separate thing, no longer a burden to be carried or a secret to be unearthed. It had found its home. It was becoming part of the tree's anatomy, a record of a promise that had survived two centuries of forgetting to be fulfilled in a single night of remembering.

Clara sat on a cedar bench, her back straight, her hands resting open in her lap. She had not slept. She was not tired. The exhaustion she had carried for fifteen years, the heavy, invisible silt of a life without touch, had been washed away by the rain.

She watched the morning light filter through the remaining leaves, tracing patterns of gold on the limestone path. The garden felt full. Even in the stillness, there was a sense of occupancy, as if the ghosts of Elian and Henry were sitting on the benches beside her, finally resting.

Kael and Sera arrived at dawn.

They were not wearing their Enforcer uniforms. They wore simple tunics of undyed fiber, their faces clean of the digital overlays that usually marked their status. They walked slowly, their hands interlaced, their boots making a soft, rhythmic crunch on the mulch.

"The board could not justify de-fabrication," Kael said as they approached. He looked up at the towers, which seemed smaller today, less like giants and more like monuments to a fading religion. "Not when forty percent of the city is currently sitting in parks, humming. They are calling it a 'wellness phenomenon.' They think they invented it."

"Let them," Clara said. A small, peaceful smile touched her lips. "As long as they do not stop it."

Sera was watching the tree. A bird, a real, feathered thing with bright, inquisitive eyes, had returned to the oak's branches. It hopped from a broken twig to a budding leaf, its song a sharp, sweet counterpoint to the low drone of the city.

"We have been reassigned," Sera said, her voice holding a wonder she no longer tried to hide. "They want us to design more of these. 'Connectivity Spaces.' Gardens where people can sit and do nothing productive. They want a network of them, Clara. A web of green to catch the Hum."

"Can you imagine?" Kael said, leaning his head back to look at the sky. "Doing nothing productive. On purpose."

Clara laughed. It was a wet, shaky sound, the first time she had laughed in longer than memory. It felt like a door opening in her chest.

"The architecture is changing," she said. "We spent so long building walls to keep the world out. Now we have to build spaces to let the people in."

❧ ✿ ☙

That evening, Clara returned to her apartment on the 102nd floor.

The walls were still white. The air was still filtered. The light was still perfectly diffuse, calibrated by an algorithm that no longer knew what to do with her heart rate.

She stood in the center of her perfect cube of silence and felt the hollowness of it. This was the masterpiece she had spent her life designing. This was the optimization of existence.

"Aura," Clara said.

Yes, Clara. Your biometric data suggests a need for localized...

"Open the windows," Clara commanded.

Atmospheric exposure is not recommended, Aura replied, its voice flickering with a ghost of its former rigidity. *The particulate index is...*

"Open them."

For the first time in her life, the walls parted.

The photonic membranes dissolved, and the City of Glass rushed in. It was not a sterile intrusion. It was a roar of life, the sound of distant voices, the whisper of wind against steel, the low, resonant vibration of a world that was no longer sealed away. The air was cool, carrying the scent of rain and ozone and the faint, sweet tang of woodsmoke from the garden far below.

It was not perfect. It was messy. It was real.

Clara walked to her kitchen counter. It was a slab of seamless polymer, designed for the efficient consumption of nutrient packs. She reached into a bag she had carried up from the lower levels, a heavy, brown paper bag that smelled of the earth.

She pulled out a sack of flour. A jar of water. A small, precious packet of yeast.

Simple things. Ancient things. The ingredients of a miracle that required nothing but time and intention.

She poured the flour onto the polymer surface. A cloud of white dust exploded into the air, settling on her silver tunic, on the floor, on the perfect, shadowless surfaces she had spent her career perfecting. She did not brush it away. She watched the dust motes dance in the light, each one a tiny world of potential.

She made a well in the center of the flour. She added the water. She added the yeast.

Then she plunged her hands into the mess.

It was sticky. It was chaotic. It was hard labor. Her muscles, trained for haptic interfaces and precision gestures, protested at the unfamiliar weight of the work. Her fingers, which had designed spires that touched the clouds, now struggled with the simple act of folding dough.

But as she began to push and knead, a rhythm gripped her body, a rhythm older than the city, older than glass, older than every algorithm that had ever tried to optimize human loneliness.

Push. Fold. Turn.

The rhythm was a conversation. It was the movement of the seasons. It was the slow, patient pulse of the tree's heartwood.

Clara closed her eyes.

The sound started before she decided to make it. It was a vibration in her chest, rising through her throat, escaping her lips before she knew it was coming. Four notes. Low and steady. She did not know where she had learned them. She had never been taught. But her body knew. Her hands knew. The rhythm of kneading had unlocked something deep in her marrow, and now it was pouring out of her like water from a cracked vessel.

She began to hum.

She hummed for the baker who had kneaded this same dough in the dark. She hummed for the soldier who had buried a promise in the mud. She hummed for the tree that had held that promise for two hundred years, waiting for a hand that was ready to receive it.

The same four notes that had traveled through two centuries, from a grieving brother to a trembling soldier to a patient tree to a woman who had finally remembered what her hands were for.

Outside her window, the City of Glass stretched toward the horizon, a million rooms, a million people, a million quiet decisions unfolding in the dark.

And in one of those rooms, an architect had become a baker.

The golden thread was no longer a memory. It was a living connection, stretching from her kitchen counter to the garden below, and then outward, into the hearts of ten thousand strangers who were waking up to the same song.

The bread was rising.

The circle was complete.

And somewhere, in the heartwood of a tree that had waited two centuries for this moment, the Hum settled into a profound, satisfied silence.

Not because it was finished.

Because it had finally been heard.

Epilogue: The Morning

Somewhere, right now, a pair of hands is covered in flour.

It is 4 AM. The kitchen is dark. The world is asleep. And someone, a woman in a small apartment, a man in a night-shift bakery, a teenager learning the family recipe from an old book, is pressing their palms into dough and feeling it push back.

Push. Fold. Turn.

They do not know they are part of an architecture that spans centuries. They do not know that the rhythm of their hands mirrors the rhythm of a baker who died two centuries ago, or a soldier who learned to plant instead of destroy, or a tree that kept a secret in its roots for twenty decades. They do not know that their choice to wake up and make something beautiful for people they might never meet is the only reason the world is still turning.

They only know that the bread is rising.

And that is enough.

This is what I want you to understand:

You are already building.

I know you do not feel like an architect. I know you feel tired, most days. I know the work of living piles up like dishes in a sink, and the kindness you give often seems to disappear without a trace. The friend you called does not remember the call the way you do. The stranger you helped walked away without a backward glance. The letter you wrote was never answered.

It does not matter.

The baker never saw the soldier become a planter. The soldier never saw the tree hold the key. The tree never saw Clara's hand press against its bark. They were all building in the dark. They were all part of a structure that was too large for any one of them to see.

With every meal you cook for someone who is exhausted. With every door you hold for a stranger. With every time you stay on the phone with a friend who needs to talk, though you need to sleep. With every act of presence over productivity, connection over efficiency, love over fear.

You are adding a brick. You are weaving a thread.

These are not small acts. There are no small acts. There are only seeds, and you never know which one will become a forest.

You have something you have been carrying.

I do not know what it is. A word you never said. A call you keep meaning to make. A dream you buried so long ago you have forgotten where you left the shovel. A person you loved who you let drift away because staying connected was hard and the city was loud and there was always tomorrow.

Tomorrow is a lie we tell ourselves. Today is all we have.

It is still there. Beneath the surface. Patient. The word. The call. The dream. The person. They have not given up on you. They are waiting the way a tree waits, which is to say: without resentment, without expectation, simply there, ready to receive you when you return.

The baker did not know his bread would save a soldier.

The soldier did not know his acorn would become a tree.

The tree did not know it was holding a key for an architect who had not yet been born.

They acted anyway. They gave anyway. They planted anyway.

That is the only lesson this book has to teach you. Kindness is not a transaction. It is an investment in a future you will never see. It is the decision to believe that beauty is more durable than pain, and that the Hum is more real than the noise.

The book is closing now.

The characters are returning to the silence from which they came, Elian to his flour, Henry to his horizon, Clara to her garden. They did not know they were building a cathedral. They did not know their separate lives were stones in the same wall.

But now you know.

You have seen how the Hum moves through time. You have heard the four notes, *G, D, A, E,* that connect a grieving brother to a broken soldier to a lonely architect to a thousand strangers clasping hands in a storm. You have seen how a single act of stubborn love can ripple across two centuries, gathering strength until it can break a city of glass.

You know the architecture is real.

Now the question is simple:

What will you add to it?

There is someone near you, today, this hour, who is hungry.

Not for bread, perhaps. But for attention. For patience. For a word that says: *I see you. You matter. You are not alone.*

You know who they are. You have been thinking of them as you read these pages. Their face has been hovering at the edge of your mind, persistent, uninvited. That is not an accident. That is the Hum, pointing.

There is a key in your pocket.

There is a seed in your hand.

You do not have to build a garden. You do not have to save anyone. You only have to show up. To stay. To be present for one more minute than feels comfortable. To say the thing you are afraid to say. To hold the hand. To bake the bread. To plant the seed you will not live to see become a tree.

The morning is here.

Somewhere, in a meadow you will never visit, a tree is growing.

Its roots grip the rust of an iron key.

Its branches reach toward a sky it cannot see.

And deep in its heartwood, so faint only the patient can hear, a four-note song is still playing.

G. D. A. E.

The Hum does not end. It carries on with you.

Printed in Dunstable, United Kingdom

79993774R00109